'A TOUCH OF LOVE'

Tamara has no money to support
her young nephew and two small
nieces after their father and mother
have been drowned. The Solicitor
tells her the only possible thing to
do is to take them to their natural
guardian, the Duke of Granchester.

Apart from hating the Duke for the
way he treated his brother when he
married, Tamara has made him the
villain in a novel she has written.

Saying she is the governess of the
children she goes to the Castle and
finds the Duke is almost as unpleasant
as she has depicted him.

How, after defying the Duke in many
different ways she saves him from
being paralysed, is told in this exciting,
dramatic 204th book by Barbara
Cartland.

Also by BARBARA CARTLAND

Books of Love, Life and Health
THE YOUTH SECRET
THE MAGIC OF HONEY
THE MAGIC OF HONEY COOK BOOK
THE FASCINATING FORTIES
MEN ARE WONDERFUL
FOOD FOR LOVE
LOVE, LIFE AND SEX
RECIPES FOR LOVERS

Historical Biography
THE OUTRAGEOUS QUEEN
THE PRIVATE LIFE OF CHARLES II
THE SCANDALOUS LIFE OF KING CAROL
METTERNICH
DIANE DE POITIERS

Romances
THE MAGNIFICENT MARRIAGE
THE KARMA OF LOVE
THE MASK OF LOVE
A SWORD TO THE HEART
BEWITCHED
THE IMPETUOUS DUCHESS
SHADOW OF SIN
THE GLITTERING LIGHTS
THE DEVIL IN LOVE
THE TEARS OF LOVE
A DREAM FROM THE NIGHT
NEVER LAUGH AT LOVE
THE PROUD PRINCESS
THE SECRET OF THE GLEN
THE HEART TRIUMPHANT
HUNGRY FOR LOVE
THE DISGRACEFUL DUKE
VOTE FOR LOVE
A DUEL WITH DESTINY
PUNISHMENT OF A VIXEN
NO ESCAPE FROM LOVE
BARS OF IRON
THE SONS OF THE SHEIK
VICISSITUDES OF EVANGELINE
MAN AND MAID
THE LOVE PIRATE

General
BARBARA CARTLAND'S BOOK OF USELESS INFORMATION

and published by CORGI BOOKS

A Touch of Love

Barbara Cartland

CORGI BOOKS
A DIVISION OF TRANSWORLD PUBLISHERS LTD

A TOUCH OF LOVE

A CORGI BOOK 0 552 10744 1

First publication in Great Britain

PRINTING HISTORY
Corgi edition published 1978

This book is set in Times 10/12pt.

Corgi Books are published by Transworld Publishers Ltd.,
Century House, 61–63 Uxbridge Road, Ealing, London, W5 5SA

Made and printed in Great Britain by
Richard Clay (The Chaucer Press), Ltd., Bungay, Suffolk.

A TOUCH OF LOVE

CHAPTER ONE
1820

"I am afraid, Miss Selincourt, that I have bad news for you!"

"Oh, no! I was hoping you would not say that!"

"I assure you I have done everything in my power and spent many sleepless nights worrying as to how I could have something different to report, but it is hopeless."

Mr. Lawson, the senior partner of Lawson, Cresey and Houghton, had a note of sincerity in his voice which was unmistakable.

The girl to whom he was speaking gave a deep sigh and sat down in the chair opposite him, her eyes large and worried in her oval face as she asked:

"Are things really . . . bad?"

Mr. Lawson gave her a look of sympathy before he replied:

"You shall judge for yourself."

A grey-haired man of about fifty, he had to put on his spectacles before he could find the paper he wanted amongst a number of others on his desk.

Then he held it in front of him, obviously reading it over to himself as if he hoped by doing so he might find some salient point he had missed.

Finally he laid it down and said:

"You know, Miss Selincourt, that I had a great admiration for your brother-in-law, Lord Ronald, and I was very proud that he extended to me his friendship."

Tamara Selincourt nodded and he went on:

"I begged him on numerous occasions to make some provision in the event of his death, but he merely laughed at me."

"But why should he have expected to die?" Tamara asked. "After all, he was only thirty-three and my sister was just six months younger."

"Thirty-three!" Mr. Lawson repeated to himself. "You are right, Miss Selincourt, at thirty-three one does not think about death."

"And their new boat was considered to be especially sea-worthy," Tamara cried. "After all, it cost a great deal of money."

"I am well aware of that," Mr. Lawson answered, "and it is one of the things which now have to be paid for."

"Ronald thought that he might make a little money out of her, perhaps taking a cargo from one harbour to another."

Tamara spoke almost as if she was speaking to herself and unexpectedly she laughed.

"That was really nonsense, as we both know! Ronald and my sister just loved the sea. They were only happy when they were sailing over the waves, setting out on what seemed to them an exciting adventure and . . . leaving us . . . behind."

Tamara's voice dropped on the last words. Then she added hardly above a whisper:

"What will . . . become of the . . . children?"

"That is what has concerned me," Mr. Lawson replied. "After all Sándor is nearly twelve and should soon be going to school."

"He is a very bright boy," Tamara said. "In fact they are all unusually intelligent, which is not surprising when you remember how clever my father was."

"I have always regretted that I never had the pleasure of meeting him," Mr. Lawson answered.

"He was brilliant!" Tamara exclaimed, "and although his books did not make very much money they will always be re-printed for the use of scholars."

"I am sure of that," Mr. Lawson agreed, "and because I am also sure Sándor has inherited his grandfather's brains he must be well educated. There is only one way that can be accomplished."

"How?" Tamara asked.

She raised her eyes to Mr. Lawson's as she spoke, and he thought, as he had thought many times before, how lovely she was.

She certainly had a beauty not usually found in a small Cornish village.

"She is like an exotic orchid," he told himself and wondered how many young men, if they had the opportunity, would think the same.

Tamara certainly did not look English.

Her red hair, such a dark, rich auburn that it could only have come from South-East Europe, framed the perfect oval of her face and gave her skin a translucent whiteness which again was very un-English.

Her eyes were so dark as to be almost purple, and yet Mr. Lawson could not help thinking that despite her exotic appearance there was something very young and very innocent about her.

"How old are you, Miss Selincourt?" he asked unexpectedly.

She smiled at him.

"I thought that was a question you should never ask a lady," she replied. "To be truthful I am nineteen, thirteen years younger than my sister, Maïka, but then there was a brother in between us who died when he was only a child."

"Nineteen!" Mr. Lawson repeated to himself. "You are too young, if I may say so, to have so much responsibility thrust upon you."

11

"But I have to look after the children. Who else is there?" Tamara asked. "And anyway, I love them and they love me."

She looked at the worried expression on Mr. Lawson's face and said:

"I am prepared to work for them, to do anything that is necessary; but I was hoping you would tell me there is enough money left so that in the meantime we should not starve."

"I know that is what you hoped, Miss Selincourt," Mr. Lawson replied, "but, unfortunately..."

"I made £40 out of the first book I wrote," Tamara interrupted. "It seemed a lot at the time, but I am very hopeful that my second one, which is now in the Publishers' hands, will make me a great deal more."

"When is it to be published?" Mr. Lawson asked.

"Any day now. They did not give me an exact date, but they told me it would be some time in June."

Mr. Lawson looked down at the piece of paper that was in front of him, before he said:

"Supposing you make another £40, or even double that amount, you still could not keep yourself and three children on such a small sum."

There was silence. Then Tamara said:

"Are you telling me there is no other money?"

"That is the truth."

She stared at him incredulously.

"But how . . . I do not understand?"

"The allowance your brother-in-law, Lord Ronald Grant, received every quarter ends with his death, and I am afraid that the last amount which arrived a week ago has already been anticipated."

"To pay for the boat!"

"Exactly!"

"But the house . . . ?"

12

"The house, as I expect you know, is mortgaged and you are extremely fortunate in that there is a purchaser ready to buy it."

Tamara looked at the solicitor in a startled manner.

"But . . . I thought we could . . . stay here."

"You must see that is impossible," Mr. Lawson said. "The house was always too big and too expensive for Lord Ronald's means, but he and your sister fell in love with it and believed they could make ends meet."

Tamara was silent.

She knew only too well how both her sister and her brother-in-law were prepared always to leave everything to chance, good luck, or just hope.

She had had a suspicion for some years that they were running more and more hopelessly into debt.

But Lord Ronald had insisted on building a new boat because their old one was unseaworthy, and he blithely ignored the question of how he was to pay for it.

Now a storm had brought catastrophe and tragedy to them all.

Lord Ronald Grant and his wife had been drowned when a sudden and unexpected tempest had burst out of what seemed a cloudless sky.

The 'Sea Lark' had been swept away to be wrecked, they learnt later, on the rocks.

The shock had been all the more terrible because it was two days before Tamara could learn what had happened.

She only felt within herself that the worst had occurred when her sister and her husband did not return.

Some fishermen had gone out as soon as the storm had abated, but all they had discovered were fragments of the 'Sea Lark' floating on the waves and, pathetically, a little woollen cap which had belonged to Lady Ronald.

It had all happened so unexpectedly, so suddenly that it was hard for Tamara to realise that her good-tempered,

13

charming brother-in-law was dead and that she would never see again her sister, whom she adored.

Now, as if her thoughts went to what Mr. Lawson had been saying a little earlier on, she said aloud:

"They gave me a home after Papa died. I was so happy with them, and you know, Mr. Lawson, if it is the last thing I do I have to repay that debt."

There was a note in Tamara's voice which showed she was not very far from tears, and after a moment Mr. Lawson said:

"I understand only too well what you are feeling, Miss Selincourt, and that is why you will appreciate that the only sensible course for you to take is the one I am about to suggest to you."

"What is that?" Tamara asked curiously.

"It is," he said slowly, "that you should take the children to their uncle, the Duke of Granchester!"

If he had exploded a bomb in front of her Tamara could not have looked more astonished.

"Take them to the Duke?" she repeated, her voice incredulous. "How could you suggest such a thing?"

"Who else is there?" Mr. Lawson asked. "As far as I know your brother-in-law has not kept in touch with any member of his family, and the children are undoubtedly, now they are orphans, His Grace's responsibility."

"It is impossible!" Tamara protested. "Surely you are aware of the manner in which the Duke has treated his brother . . . and my sister?"

There was an unmistakable note of hostility in her voice and Mr. Lawson said quietly:

"I know the story only too well, but we cannot entirely blame the present Duke for his father's attitude when Lord Ronald wished to marry your sister."

"It was inhuman! Barbaric!" Tamara stormed, and now her dark eyes were flashing. "Do you know what happened,

14

Mr. Lawson, when Ronald wrote to his father to say he wanted to marry Maïka?"

Mr. Lawson did not reply and she went on angrily:

"He stormed down to Oxford where Ronald was in residence and told him that if he married Maïka he would never speak to him again!"

"You must understand," Mr. Lawson said mildly, "that the Duke, who was a very pious man, had a horror of anything connected with the play-house!"

"He said because Maïka appeared on the stage that she was an actress. But in fact she was nothing of the sort!"

Tamara's voice seemed to ring out as she continued:

"Maïka was a singer and because at the time my mother was desperately ill and my father could not afford the high fees asked by the best doctors, she sang in an Opera Company."

Mr. Lawson was about to speak but Tamara went on:

"In two years she made enough money to pay for all the treatments my mother required."

"Surely this was explained to His Grace at the time?" Mr. Lawson murmured.

"Do you suppose he would listen?" Tamara asked furiously. "He would not even allow Ronald to speak in my sister's defence."

She drew in her breath before she said:

"Ronald told me that he spoke as if Maïka was a prostitute, a woman beyond the pale, whom he had picked up in some gutter! He would neither meet her nor hear about her. He just repeated his ultimatum!"

She paused before she added:

"When Ronald told him that, whatever he said, he intended to marry my sister, the Duke walked out and never spoke to him again!"

She threw out her hands as she asked:

"What sort of father was that? What sort of man is it who

15

would repudiate his own son without allowing him even to speak a word in his own defence?"

"The Duke has been dead for some time," Mr. Lawson remarked quietly.

"The present Duke is no better," Tamara snapped. "He is only a year older than Ronald and you would think he might have understood and perhaps sympathised! But he slavishly accepted his father's decision that the family should sever all connections with the 'black sheep'."

Her voice broke on the last word.

She rose and walked to the window to stare out fighting her tears before she said:

"You know how sweet, gentle and wonderful in every way my sister was. Actually she hated the stage and everything to do with it."

"She once told me so," Mr. Lawson replied.

"As soon as she made enough money to save my mother," Tamara went on as if he had not spoken, "she left the Theatre just to be Ronald's wife, as she had always wanted to be, and they were blissfully happy."

"I do not think I have ever known a couple who were so happy," Mr. Lawson agreed almost enviously.

"And they died together," Tamara murmured. "I do not think either of them could have gone on living alone."

Mr. Lawson adjusted his spectacles.

"Now to get back to where we started, Miss Selincourt," he said briskly, "and that is the financial position of you and the children. The only possible thing to do is to take them where they belong."

"Do you really think I would do that?" Tamara asked. "That I would humiliate myself and them, to ask favours of a man who has behaved so abominably to his own brother?"

"What is the alternative?" Mr. Lawson asked.

"There must be something . . . something we could . . . do," Tamara said desperately.

16

She walked back towards the desk and sat down in the chair in which she had been sitting before, almost as if her legs would no longer support her.

"If there is, I have no idea of it," Mr. Lawson said. "Quite frankly, Miss Selincourt, I think it only right and just that the Duke should be made responsible for his brother's children."

Tamara did not speak and after a moment he went on:

"Mr. Trevena says he will take over the house and pay enough money to rid you of the mortgage and all Lord Ronald's other debts, provided he has possession immediately."

"I suppose he wants it for his son who is getting married," Tamara said dully.

"That is right," Mr. Lawson replied. "He is a difficult man, and if we put him off he may buy a house elsewhere."

Tamara was silent, realising that to sell a house of the size of the Manor in that isolated part of Cornwall was not easy.

They might go for months, if not years, without finding another buyer, and it would be impossible to feed the children, let alone provide them with clothes, and education.

"Is the Duke aware that his brother is dead?" she asked after a moment.

Mr. Lawson looked slightly uncomfortable before he said:

"I have not yet informed His Grace."

Tamara looked at him Then suddenly there was a little light in her eyes.

"I know why . . . because you were waiting for Ronald's allowance to come in. That was kind of you . . . very kind."

"And strictly unethical!" Mr. Lawson said with a smile.

There was silence for a moment, before Tamara asked:

"Must we tell him . . . now?"

"I am afraid so," Mr. Lawson replied. "You would not wish me to behave in such an illegal manner that I should no longer be allowed to practise as a Solicitor."

"No, of course not," Tamara answered, "and you have been so kind already. I am sure my brother-in-law never paid your firm for the many times he had to consult you over the many documents appertaining to the Estate and of course the boat."

"It is not of any great consequence," Mr. Lawson replied. "As I have said, I valued your brother-in-law's friendship and I do not think anyone could have known your sister without loving her."

"It is a pity the Grant family could not hear you say that," Tamara observed.

"Would you think me very impertinent, Miss Selincourt, if I suggested that when you meet the Duke of Granchester you do not fight old battles," Mr. Lawson asked. "Content yourself with trying to make him interested in the three orphans and accept them as his sole responsibility?"

"Supposing he refuses to do anything for them?" Tamara asked. "It is quite likely, considering they are my sister's children."

"I cannot believe that the Duke would allow anyone with the name of Grant to starve," Mr. Lawson replied. "Furious though the old Duke was with Lord Ronald, he continued his allowance all these years."

"The same allowance he made him when he was an under-graduate at Oxford," Tamara said scornfully.

"It was nevertheless a substantial one," Mr. Lawson insisted, "and the Duke could in fact have cut his son off with only the proverbial penny."

"If you think I am going to be grateful to the family . . . I am not!" Tamara said in a hard voice. "As for the present Duke, from all I have heard about him . . ."

She gave a sudden cry and put her fingers up to her lips.

"What is it?" Mr. Lawson asked in astonishment.

"I have just remembered . . . I did not think of it until now, but I cannot . . . I cannot take the children to the Duke of

Granchester. If they go, they must go . . . without me!"

"But why?" Mr. Lawson asked.

"Because I have . . . based my . . . novel on him!"

"On the Duke?"

Tamara put her hand up to her forehead as if she was trying to think clearly.

"You remember my first book, which although it was a fairy-story was also slightly satirical?"

"Indeed I thought it very amusing and original," Mr. Lawson said.

"Well, this book, the one which is being published at the moment, is a novel about a spiteful, unkind, wicked Duke, who is in fact the present Duke of Granchester!"

"But you have never seen him, and you know nothing about him."

"I know all that Ronald has told me, and because I was interested I always looked for anything written about him in the newspapers and magazines."

She looked at Mr. Lawson in consternation as she went on:

"When Ronald's friends whom he had met at Oxford came to stay with us, they always told us stories about the Duke and I stored them up in my memory."

"And you think the Duke would recognise himself?" Mr. Lawson asked. "In which case your book might be libellous."

"I do not think he would care to acknowledge the portrait as a true one," Tamara answered. "I have no reason to think he would even read it, but . . ."

She was silent and after a moment Mr. Lawson said:

"Exactly what have you said that could identify His Grace as being the character portrayed in your novel?"

"Well, for one thing the book is called 'The Ducal Wasp' and the Duke is the villain who goes about making everybody miserable and unhappy. He drives Phaetons and Curricles which are always black and yellow, and his servants wear a black and yellow livery."

"Which are the Grant family colours," Mr. Lawson said.

"Exactly!" Tamara answered, "and, oh, there are lots of other things about him which Ronald told me and about the Castle. There are also incidents I have invented like a race meeting where the villain pulls the favourite so that he can make a lot of money by betting on another horse from his stables, which of course wins."

Mr. Lawson put his hand up to his forehead.

"Why did you not let me read it before you sent it to the Publishers? You will undoubtedly be prosecuted for libel and ordered to pay enormous damages."

Tamara laughed.

"That is easy, at any rate. If I have no money, I cannot pay."

"Then you may go to prison."

"Then I will plead that every word I wrote was true and therefore justified."

Mr. Lawson groaned.

"That is something which cannot happen! You will sit down, Miss Selincourt, here and now, and write to the Publishers withdrawing your book!"

"Withdraw my book?" Tamara cried. "I shall do nothing of the sort!"

"You must! You must see it is the only possible course for you to take," Mr. Lawson insisted.

He saw the light of defiance in Tamara's eyes and said quietly:

"You have to think of the children. Knowing what you believe the Duke to be like, could you bear to send them alone to Granchester Castle? I know they would be unhappy without you."

There was a long silence. Then Tamara capitulated.

"No, you are right. I will send the letter."

20

"I will draft it for you," Mr. Lawson said. "In the meantime, I will despatch a letter to-morrow morning to the Duke, informing him of his brother's death and telling him that the children will arrive at the beginning of next week."

"As soon as . . . that?"

"We have to remember Mr. Trevena."

"Y.yes . . . of course."

Once again Tamara rose to walk to the window.

"I am thinking," she said, "that if I must . . . go with them, and I realise that Vava is too young to go without me, then it might be best not to go as . . . Maïka's sister."

Mr. Lawson considered for a moment what she had said. Then he said:

"No, of course not, I should have thought of that. It would be best to say that you have looked after them as . . ."

". . . as a Governess," Tamara interposed. "At least then he will have to give me my wages, so that I shall not be entirely dependent upon him."

Mr. Lawson looking at her and seeing the sunshine touch the dark red of her hair to a flaming gold, thought she would look very unlike the usual run of Governesses to be found in charge of small children.

He did not however express his thoughts, he only asked aloud:

"What name shall I call you?"

"Does it matter?" Tamara asked. "No, wait, it had better be something that the children can remember."

"Why not Miss Wynne?"

"Excellent. I will tell them that is what we are going to do."

"But I hope you will not try and win a battle against the Duke," Mr. Lawson said. "It is important, Miss Selincourt, that he should like the children. He is a very rich and powerful man, and there is nothing he could not do for them if he takes a fancy to them."

21

"I think he is far more likely to fling us all into a dungeon and keep us there on bread and water until we die," Tamara said dramatically.

Mr. Lawson laughed.

"I think if that was discovered it would cause a scandal which would reverberate throughout the whole country! I assure you that from what I have heard of the Duke he does not like scandals."

"No, of course not," Tamara agreed. "That is what his father thought Ronald was causing by marrying an actress."

There was no mistaking the bitterness in her tone and Mr. Lawson said quickly:

"I do beg of you to try to forget the past. As close relatives of His Grace, the children cannot only have everything they have ever desired, but also a unique opportunity for happiness in the future."

Tamara did not speak and after a moment he said:

"It seems strange that we should be talking about it now when Kadine is only ten, but in seven years time she will be a débutante and a very beautiful one. The whole social world will be open to her and her sister as the nieces of His Grace the Duke of Granchester."

Tamara looked at him in surprise, then with a quick change of mood which Mr. Lawson knew was characteristic of her, she said:

"You are right! Of course you are right, and I must think of the girls. They will both be very beautiful, as you say, and perhaps they will be able to pick and choose the right sort of husbands . . . men who are rich but whom they also love."

There was a sudden softness in her dark eyes which made Mr. Lawson think to himself that long before Kadine and her little sister Validé were grown up, their aunt would be married, or at least she would have had the opportunity of it not once but a hundred times.

He rose from his desk.

"If you will wait a few minutes, Miss Selincourt, I will draft a letter for you to write to your Publishers, and also a letter from myself to His Grace telling him to expect you."

"I will wait," Tamara said.

Mr. Lawson smiled at her and went to the outer office where there were several clerks sitting at their high desks, their white quill pens moving busily over the books and documents which proved Lawson, Cresey and Houghton one of the busiest Solicitors in the town.

Tamara rose from the chair in which she had been sitting and once again walked to the window.

She felt as if everything that had happened this morning was going round and round in her head in a manner which made it hard for her to think straight.

For one thing it was more of a blow than she was willing to express to Mr. Lawson to know that she must withdraw her novel.

She had had such high hopes of making quite a considerable sum of money from it, considering how much she had made with her first book.

That had been a very slim volume, but the Publishers had sent her several reviews which had been complimentary.

She thought that a novel might capture the imagination of the smart social world that had made a hero out of Sir Walter Scott and a great financial success of Lord Byron.

Hers combined adventure, villainy and a certain amount of romance in what she had thought was an agreeable mixture which should please almost everybody's taste.

Living so quietly in Cornwall, she had had little opportunity of meeting social celebrities.

But her imagination had been excited by the tales of the cruel, unpleasant Duke of Granchester who had ostracised his brother as his father had done before him.

Tamara had adored her brother-in-law, and every time she dipped her pen in the ink to write something scathing and vitriolic about the villain in her novel, she felt she was somehow paying back the Duke for his unkindness.

She had deliberately not shown Lord Ronald her manuscript before it went to the Publishers.

He was such a good-humoured, gentle person that she felt he might have protested against the picture she had drawn of his brother, even though there was no reason for him to defend any member of his family.

They had certainly treated him as if he were a pariah, an out-cast, and yet, though he often laughed about their various eccentricities, he had never been unkind.

"I cannot understand," Tamara's sister Maïka had once said to her, "how they could bear to lose Ronald. He is so charming, so kind and so sympathetic you would think he must have left a great void in his family which no-one else could fill."

"They are stiff-necked, autocratic and altogether contemptible!" Tamara had answered, but Maïka had merely laughed at her.

"I do not mind being outside the Castle gates," she answered. "It is just that sometimes I hate to think that Ronald cannot afford the horses he ought to ride, or the clothes he ought to wear, or be able to attend the races at Newmarket and Ascot."

"I have never seen anybody so happy as Ronald," Tamara answered. "It does not matter what clothes he wears down here, and I believe he is just as amused by racing the children on the sands as he would be watching a jockey come in first carrying his colours at Newmarket."

Her sister had kissed her.

"You are such a comfort to me, Tamara," she said. "Sometimes I feel it is wrong that I should have deprived Ronald of so much, but as far as I am concerned in him I had the whole world and Heaven in my arms."

Tamara had only to see her brother-in-law and sister

together to know that Mr. Lawson was right when he said it would be impossible for two people to be happier than they were.

There seemed to be a light in their eyes when they looked at each other that held a radiance which was not of this world.

If Ronald had been away from her for a few hours Maïka would be waiting for him when he returned, to throw herself into his arms and pull his head down to hers.

They would kiss each other closely and passionately as if they had only just fallen in love and the wonder of it was irresistible.

But now they were both gone and Tamara knew, as if it were a sacred trust, the children were in her care and there was no-one else to love them or to look after them except herself.

'Mr. Lawson is right,' she thought. 'The Duke must think of me as the children's Governess and as he will surely not wish to be bothered with finding anyone else, he will be content to keep me on in such a position.'

Mr. Lawson came back into the room.

"Here is the letter to your Publishers," he said. "It is quite brief and to the point, and I have asked if they will send the manuscript to this office. It will be safer here. If you left it lying about at Granchester Castle it might be uncomfortable for you."

Tamara turned and slowly walked to the desk and as he saw the expression on her face Mr. Lawson said:

"I am sorry. I know this represents for you a lot of wasted work, but it is really the only thing you can do."

As Tamara picked up a pen, he went on:

"You must write another book, and perhaps you will find something pleasant to write about at Granchester Castle – even its owner!"

"If wishes were horses, beggars might ride!" Tamara

answered and laughed.

She signed the letter and put the big quill pen back in the pen-holder.

"I shall try to forget it," she said, "but I suppose every author feels when publishing a book that they have produced a baby. I cannot help mourning my poor little still-born child."

Mr. Lawson laughed but he said

"That Miss Selincourt, is the sort of remark you should certainly not make at Granchester Castle. It would undoubtedly shock the elderly Grant relations."

"I shall guard both my tongue and my pen," Tamara promised, "and my next manuscript will come here to you. You shall cut out every libellous word in it before it goes to the Publishers."

"I shall keep you to that promise," Mr. Lawson smiled. "I have no wish, Miss Selincourt, to have to defend you in court."

"And I have no wish to see the inside of a Debtors' Prison," Tamara replied.

"I will send this letter and the one to the Duke to-day," Mr. Lawson said, "and I will come over to the Manor the day after tomorrow to see if I can help you with your packing. By then I shall have made arrangements for your journey."

"You are very kind."

She put out both her hands towards him.

"I know that Ronald and my sister would want me to thank you for the friendship you have shown me and the children."

Mr. Lawson held both Tamara's hands very tightly. Then he said:

"You are being very brave, my dear. I only wish I could have had better news for you, but perhaps, who knows, it will all turn out for the best."

"If it is the best for the children, then I shall be content," Tamara said. "As far as I am concerned, if I am honest, I am apprehensive of what awaits us at Granchester Castle."

Riding back on the old horse which had served the family well for many seasons, Tamara felt the wind from the sea blowing on her face and thought she would always be home-sick for the beauty of Cornwall.

She had come to live with her sister after their father died and found the wild beauty of the furthermost point of England so lovely and so unlike anything she had ever seen before that she had not missed the crowded, busy life she had left in Oxford.

She was just fifteen when her father, Conrad Selincourt died of a heart-attack.

She had looked after him during the last years when he had been alone without her mother and she was therefore older in her ways and in her outlook than most girls of her age.

She was also a great deal better educated.

Living at Oxford, the daughter of a Don, she had been acquainted with and listened to a great number of men as intelligent and cultured as her father.

Besides which she had studied and had access to fine Libraries ever since she was old enough to learn.

If Conrad Selincourt had given his daughters his brains, their mother had undoubtedly contributed their beauty.

It was not only Maïka's voice which had gained her a place in an Opera Company but also her beauty.

It had in fact been her teacher at Oxford who had secured her position and seen to it that she was given a salary which far exceeded what she might have expected as an amateur with no experience.

The Opera Company was not the usual impecunious company which toured from city to city, but was financed privately by a Committee of benevolent Music Lovers who thought it important that people outside London should

27

have the opportunity to hear good music.

It was when they were performing at Oxford that one of the leading ladies was taken ill and Maïka had the chance to take her place.

She not only sang outstandingly well but she also looked so lovely that it was obvious to the Producer and the Manager that she was just the person to fill the gap in their company.

For the Duke of Granchester to speak of her as being "a common actress and little better than a prostitute" was a gross insult and completely inaccurate.

All the ladies in the Company were in fact models of virtue, and the Committee who watched very closely over the affairs of their performers would not have tolerated licence of any sort.

Maïka, who sang at places like Bath, Tunbridge Wells and some of the lesser cities, was as untouched and unaffected by what was spoken of as a loose theatrical life as if she were a closely chaperoned débutante.

Whenever she was not actually performing she returned home, and it was in her father's house at Oxford that Lord Ronald met her and fell immediately head-over-heels in love.

That he was not yet twenty-one was sufficient excuse for his father to deprecate such an early marriage.

But the Duke, in trying to break off the attachment, was so tactless and so unnecessarily unpleasant that it achieved the very effect he wished to avoid of precipitating Lord Ronald into marriage.

Faced with the ultimatum of 'never speaking to that woman again', no young man with any spirit could have accepted it without besmirching his own honour and self-respect.

The Duke had stormed back to London and Lord Ronald had married Maïka the following month.

She finished her contract with the Opera Company, then

as Lord Ronald had taken his final examinations they had left together to seek a place where they could live.

Because they found they both had a passion for the sea, it was obvious that their home must be at the sea-side, and someone had told them that Cornwall was cheap.

They had gone there to find it, as Lord Ronald had said, the Eden they both desired and no Adam and Eve could have been happier.

The Manor was certainly very attractive, Tamara thought as she arrived home, and she felt a pang of distress to think that they must leave it as well as all the memories she had shared there with her sister and brother-in-law.

As the sounds of her horse's hoofs clattered outside the front door the children came running out.

Sándor was first, running to the horse's head and saying as he did so:

"I will take Firefly round to the stables, Aunt Tamara."

"You are very late, Aunt Tamara," Kadine said, while Validé who was five and who was always called Vava, standing at the top of the steps merely cried:

"I want my tea! You are late! I want my tea!"

"You shall have it in a moment, pet," Tamara said, picking her up in her arms. Then followed by Kadine she went into the kitchen.

There was an old woman there who helped in the house with the children and with everything else that was required.

"Ye're back, Miss Tamara," she said as Tamara entered carrying Vava in her arms.

"Yes, I am back, Lucy," Tamara answered. "Can we have tea? As Vava said I am late."

"They wouldn't eat without ye, Miss," Lucy answered, "even when I tells them there were hot scones and cream for ye all."

"It would have been greedy not to wait for you, Aunt Tamara," Kadine said.

At ten she already showed promise of a beauty which would undoubtedly make dozens of young men's hearts miss a beat once she was grown up.

Strangely enough, Tamara thought, none of the children had the dark red hair of their mother which had been a crowning glory handed down from their Hungarian grandmother.

They were all fair like their father, but Kadine and Vava had eyes with long dark lashes that made people look at them, then look again in astonishment.

Sándor's hair was more brown than gold, but he had his father's clear-cut features and was undoubtedly an extremely handsome little boy.

Looking at him when he came in from having taken the horse to the stables, Tamara thought how closely he resembled his father and wondered if there was also a resemblance to his uncle.

In which case, if the Duke of Granchester was outstandingly handsome, the portrait of him in her novel had been incorrect.

It was impossible for her to allow the villain to be too good-looking. He had to have a sardonic, cynical expression which proclaimed his wickedness at first sight.

'Anyway, I shall soon be able to judge for myself what he really looks like,' Tamara thought.

She felt her heart sink at the news she had to tell the children as soon as tea was finished.

CHAPTER TWO

Tamara had not realised there were so many people to whom she would have to say good-bye.

As soon as it was learnt locally that she and the children were leaving the Manor, the friends they had made over the years called hourly to bid them 'God-speed'.

There were a few local dignitaries from the County, but the majority were fisher-folk, farmers and villagers, who all expressed with deep sincerity how sad it was to see them go.

Over and over again as the visitors said something touching about her sister and Lord Ronald, Tamara felt the tears gather in her eyes and, when finally they were driven away from the Manor by Mr. Lawson in the gig pulled by their old horse, she could barely get a last glimpse of it through her tears.

Mr. Lawson had arranged that he would drive them into Truro in their own conveyance, and from there they would take a stagecoach to carry them on the first stage of their journey to Granchester Castle in Gloucestershire.

As they set off the children were excited at the thought of travelling and Vava did not understand that they were leaving the place that had been their home all their lives.

They had, Tamara thought, an enormous amount of luggage, not only because she had added her sister's clothes to her own, but also because she could not bear to leave behind many little objects she had known ever since she had lived in her brother-in-law's house.

There were snuff-boxes, not of any particular value, but which he had treasured; there was a work-basket belonging to her sister, and there were pieces of embroidery that they had done together.

There were even things like a very special shell the children had picked up on the sea-shore and a flag that had floated behind Lord Ronald's first boat, all mementoes of happiness.

Because she realised that in the future she was going to be very poor, and any money she had must be kept for the children in case the Duke was not as generous as Mr. Lawson hoped, she was determined to spend as little as possible on herself.

She therefore did not buy mourning and, while Sándor wore a black armband, she and the girls only added black sashes to their ordinary gowns and black ribbons to their bonnets.

Actually, with her red hair and the children's fair curls, black was exceedingly becoming and threw into prominence the clearness of their skins.

But Tamara was at the moment not concerned about her appearance although she was quite well aware that before she reached the Castle she must, as a Governess, make every effort to look subdued and perhaps dowdy.

As they drove along in the gig, Mr. Lawson tried to cheer them all up with stories that he had heard of the magnificence of Granchester Castle, and also of Granchester House in London.

"Of course the Duke is often in waiting on the King," he said, "although I cannot believe that he approves of the raffish life His Majesty enjoyed when he was the Prince of Wales."

Tamara did not answer.

For the moment she only felt the idea of meeting the Duke hanging over her like a menacing cloud.

She had hated him for the manner in which he had treated her brother-in-law and she now hated him on her own account because in a way he had been instrumental in preventing her novel from being published.

'I must write another book,' she thought.

But for the moment her mind was blank. All she could think of was the misery of leaving behind everything that was familiar and the happiness which had made her and her sister so close to each other.

The day before they left, despite the thousands of things there were to be done, Tamara had gone to the Church-yard to say a last farewell to her brother-in-law and Maïka.

Their bodies had never been found, but she had arranged with the Vicar for a plaque to their memory to be set in a special place in the Chancel.

She had asked Lucy and other women in the village who had loved them to see there were always flowers in front of it, both summer and winter.

They had promised her they would do this, and Tamara knelt in the pew where they had sat every Sunday and prayed that she would not fail her sister's trust in looking after her children.

"You must help me, Maïka," she said. "It is not going to be easy for them to remember all the things that you taught them about kindness, sympathy and understanding."

She had the feeling as she prayed that those virtues were very unlikely to be found at Granchester Castle.

When she went back to the Manor it was to find Sándor almost in tears because he had only just realised that his pony would not be able to go with them.

"He will be well looked after, Sándor," she told him, "and there will be plenty of horses for you to ride at the Castle."

"I want my own Rufus," Sándor answered. "You know, Aunt Tamara, I have had him ever since he was a foal."

"I know, dearest," Tamara answered, "but I promise you

33

he will be well looked after in the home Mr. Lawson has found for him."

As Sándor still looked so depressed she said:

"Perhaps later we could ask your uncle if we could buy him back for you."

"Do you think he would agree to that?" Sándor asked, a new light in his eyes.

"We can but try," Tamara answered.

But as she spoke she could not help thinking that if the stories of the Duke's stables were true he would hardly want a not very outstanding or well-bred pony among his pedigree stock.

There were many other crises, such as when Vava brought in a whole collection of stones from some secret place in the garden which she insisted must be included in the luggage.

And Kadine wished to take a new litter of kittens, all six of them, because she said there would be no-one to look after them properly once they had gone.

Finally they had set off, and now as they neared Truro Tamara knew they must say good-bye to their last friend in the person of Mr. Lawson.

They drew up outside the Coaching Inn, and while they were standing rather forlornly waiting for Mr. Lawson to arrange for the luggage to be put on the roof of the coach Tamara gave a sudden cry.

"Look children," she exclaimed. "There is Erth Veryon!"

They looked in the direction in which she pointed then ran across the street to where a tall man with white hair was walking hand-in-hand with a boy of about sixteen.

As they reached him Tamara said:

"Erth, it is good to see you, and I am so glad we are not leaving Cornwall without saying good-bye to you."

The man, who was about fifty years of age, put out his hand and Tamara lay her fingers into it.

He was blind, but he had a smooth unwrinkled face with

34

a remarkable expression of an inner spirituality.

"You are leaving Cornwall, Miss Tamara?" he asked.

"You recognised my voice," Tamara smiled.

"I never forget a voice," Erth Veryon replied.

"And do you remember mine?" Kadine asked.

"It is Miss Kadine!"

"And me? You remember me?" Vava questioned.

"Little Miss Vava!"

"I am here too," Sándor said. "How are you, Erth?"

"Very well, thank you, Master Sándor, and if you are setting off on your travels, I am also setting off on mine."

"Where are you going?" Tamara asked.

"I shall go where the Lord directs me."

"If He directs you to Gloucester, please come and call on us," Tamara begged. "We shall be at Granchester Castle. To see you, Erth, would be like meeting a little bit of Cornwall in a foreign land."

There was a note in her voice which made the blind man reach out again to take her hand.

"You are unhappy and worried," he said.

"Yes," she answered. "I have to take the children to live with their uncle the Duke of Granchester, and as you can guess, if it were possible, we would much rather stay here."

"I heard of Lord Ronald's death," Erth said, "and that of your sister. It was sad, very sad for you; but, you know, they are together with God."

"I hope so," Tamara said with a little quiver in her voice.

"You can believe it because it is true," Erth said in his deep Cornish voice. "But you are not only grieving for them. Something else is disturbing you."

Tamara did not think it strange or uncanny that he was so perceptive.

She had known him ever since she had lived in Cornwall and she had seen him heal her brother-in-law's broken ankle so that the doctor had been amazed that Lord Ronald was so quickly on his feet.

Erth Veryon had also healed a child in their village who had been so ill that everyone was sure he would die, and an old woman whose relatives had given her up for dead.

Holding his hand now she felt as if some vibration passed from him into her own body, and after a moment he said:

"You have hate in your heart. It will poison you. Replace it, child, with love; for only through love can you find happiness."

Tamara drew in her breath.

She might have expected that Erth would know what she was feeling. At the same time he was asking the impossible.

"You must try," he said as if she had answered him aloud. "Try to give love, then you will receive it. That is what God has promised us, and we can believe Him."

When Tamara would have answered, she heard Mr. Lawson call her from the other side of the road.

"I must go," she said. "Come and see us if ever you can, Erth."

She took her hand from his, fumbled in her hand-bag, found a half-sovereign and pressed it into the hand of Erth's grandson who was his constant companion.

As she did so she put a finger to her lips so that the boy would not thank her. Erth would never take money for his services and in consequence would often go hungry.

His grandson smiled at her and the Healer was not aware of what was happening because the children were clamouring for his attention.

"Good-bye, Erth! Good-bye!" they cried.

"Trust in God," he said to them, "and He will deliver you safely to your destination."

"We will," Kadine replied.

Then they were running across the road to Mr. Lawson.

Tamara joined them and the Solicitor hurried them into the Stage-Coach.

He had procured the best seats facing the horses for Tamara and the two girls and a place on the box with the other men for Sándor, where he much preferred to travel.

"Write to me . . . please write to me," Tamara said as she said good-bye.

"You know I will do that and I shall be waiting to hear from you."

"If it is too frightful," Tamara said in a low voice, "we shall all come back and camp in your garden or shelter in a cave on the beach."

Mr. Lawson laughed but Tamara knew he was really unhappy to see them all go.

Fortunately there was little time for long farewells as the Guard of the Stage-Coach was hurrying everyone into their places, and almost before the door was shut the horses began to move off.

The girls hung out of the window waving and shouting good-bye, but Tamara sat back in the corner of the seat and shut her eyes to prevent the tears over-flowing and running down her cheeks.

"This is really good-bye," she thought, "good-bye to the old life and Heaven knows what lies ahead in the new one."

.   .   .   .   .

It was a very long and tiring journey to Gloucester. They stayed every night at a wayside Inn and changed frequently from one Stage-Coach to another, each time with the worry of transporting their baggage and making quite sure nothing was left behind.

Tamara grew used to the surliness of porters who disliked Stage-Coaches because the passengers seldom gave large tips, and the indifference of Inn-keepers who set aside the worst rooms and the most inedible meals for those who travelled cheaply.

To the children it was an adventure.

Only on the last day, when after being held up because of

an accident on the road their coach was over three hours late, did Vava become fretful and Kadine too sleepy to take an interest in anything.

It was with a sense of apprehension that Tamara realised they would not reach the small town of Tetbury until nearly seven o'clock.

This meant, she thought, that by the time they arrived at the Castle the Duke would doubtless be at dinner, and if they interrupted his meal it would immediately start them off on the wrong foot.

She had hoped that at Tetbury there might be a carriage from the Castle to carry them the last five miles.

She had learnt from Mr. Lawson that he had not exactly asked that they should be met at Tetbury but he had informed the Duke that they would arrive there during the afternoon.

But when the Stage-Coach stopped at the rather inadequate Inn there was no sign of a private carriage, and when Tamara enquired she was told there was no-one there from the Castle.

She then had some difficulty in obtaining the hire of a chaise.

Only because the Duke's name obviously galvanised the Inn-keeper into some sort of action did he finally produce a very old vehicle drawn by an equally ancient horse.

The luggage was piled on the roof and Tamara and the children sat inside.

There was the smell of hay, old decaying leather and horse-flesh. When they set off and when the horse moved so slowly Tamara could not help thinking that he and the driver were half-asleep.

Finally after what seemed hours on the dusty road their conveyance turned in through a pair of enormous wrought-iron gates with stone lodges on each side of them.

The last part of the journey was down a most impressive

drive, flanked on either side with ancient oak-trees.

"Now we shall see the Castle!" Tamara cried with what she hoped was a gay note in her voice even though her heart felt heavy.

But only Sándor seemed interested, for the two little girls were too tired to care.

Quickly Tamara tidied their hair and straightened their bonnets, and tried to smooth the creases out of their white frocks.

She herself had spent more time than usual, on rising, in re-arranging her hair in a different style from what she had ever worn before.

She had in fact pulled it back straight from her forehead and pinned it into a bun at the back of her head.

"I must look plain and insignificant," she told herself.

However when she looked into the mirror she thought with dissatisfaction that her eyes were far too large and her lips too curved for her to look in any way an ordinary Governess.

She had chosen the very plainest of her gowns. It was a green crêpe for, as she was not supposed to be a relation, she would not be expected to wear mourning.

Tamara and Maïka had always made their own clothes and they were extremely skilful needle-women.

But Maïka had also some very lovely gowns which Lord Ronald had bought for her as presents, because he loved to see his wife looking beautiful even though she had so small an audience to admire her.

Tamara thought it was unlikely she would ever have occasion to wear the exquisite evening-gowns that her sister had possessed or the special ones that she used to wear on Sundays when she went to Church and when occasionally they entertained friends in the neighbourhood.

'When I have time,' Tamara thought looking at her own wardrobe, 'I shall make myself some severe garments in drab colours that will make me as anonymous as I wish to be.'

She was well aware that her own dresses made of light muslin or those she had copied from 'The Ladies Journal' with embroidery and small frills of lace were most unsuitable for her present position.

There had not been time after Mr. Lawson had told her they were to leave the Manor to alter anything, and the green gown which made Tamara's skin look almost dazzlingly white was in fact the plainest frock she possessed.

Even so, it could not conceal the perfection of her figure, the tininess of her waist or the soft curves of her breasts.

She changed the ribbons on her bonnet from black to green, then half-regretted that she had not left them as they were.

Then she told herself that whatever she wore it was unlikely that the Duke would condescend to notice anything so lowly as a Governess, and all she had to do was to keep in the background and be as unobtrusive as possible.

They were drawing nearer to the Castle and now Tamara could see how enormous it was.

Lord Ronald had told her that it had originally been Norman, but had been altered and built on to all through the centuries until it was a pot-pourri of many different architectural styles.

"My grandfather spent a fortune in adding new and very impressive State-Rooms," Lord Ronald said, "but he also built up the old Norman tower, repaired the Elizabethan wings and improved on the interior decorations which were made at the time of Queen Anne."

From the way her brother-in-law spoke Tamara had known that Lord Ronald loved the Castle, even though she sensed that his childhood there had not been a particularly happy one.

He never disparaged his parents, but both Maïka and Tamara were aware that they had been an austere couple who found children a nuisance and left them, where possible, in the care of servants.

"I often think that Ronald gives his own children the love he missed when he was a child," Maïka said once.

And there was no doubt that from the time Sándor was born Lord Ronald had been content to spend hours every day with the small replica of himself.

But later, Tamara thought, he loved his daughters best, while Maïka made no pretence of not putting her son first in her affection.

"He is so like you, darling," she heard her sister say once to Lord Ronald, "and how could I help loving to distraction your son simply because he is yours?"

'I must try and make up to the children for what they have lost,' Tamara thought now.

At the same time the Castle was so huge and overwhelming that she almost felt as if it came between her and her nephew and nieces and they were being separated by the very magnificence of it.

"It is very big and very old!" Sándor said as they drew up at the front door. "It ought to be filled with Knights, and there should be jousting."

Tamara was pleased that it excited his imagination, while as far as she was concerned, she could only think that it was oppressively large. She would have given everything she possessed in the whole world to turn round and go back to the cosy comfort of the Manor.

The carriage door was opened by a footman with powdered hair and she noticed that he was wearing the black and yellow livery that she had described in her novel.

Holding Vava by the hand she walked up the steps to find an elderly white-haired Butler looking at them in surprise.

"You have an appointment with His Grace, Madam?" he asked.

"His Grace is expecting us," Tamara answered. "Will you

41

inform him that his nephew and nieces have arrived?"

"His nephew and nieces?"

There was no mistaking the astonishment in the Butler's voice.

"That is what I said," Tamara replied.

She moved into the centre of the huge marble-floored Hall which had a curved staircase rising on one side of it and on the other a great mediaeval fireplace.

"I think, Madam," the Butler said in a respectful voice, "there may be some mistake. You are aware that this is the home of the Duke of Granchester?"

"I am aware of that," Tamara answered, "and as I have already told you, this is the Duke's nephew, Master Sándor Grant and his nieces, Miss Kadine and Miss Validé."

The Butler was obviously thrown into confusion by the information, but he said after a perceptible pause:

"His Grace is at dinner, Madam, but I will inform him of your arrival. Will you wait here?"

He opened a door at the far end of the Hall, showed them into a Sitting-Room, then still with a look of surprise on his face he left, closing the door behind him.

"I am tired! I want a drink!" Vava said.

"I know you do, dearest," Tamara answered, "but you will have to wait until you have seen your Uncle Howard."

"Is that what we call him?" Sándor asked, turning from his inspection of a collection of miniatures which covered a table.

"Yes . . . Uncle Howard," Tamara answered.

She lowered her voice.

"And do not forget, children, to call me Miss Wynne."

They had been practising all the days of their journey, but Tamara knew that when Vava was tired it would be difficult for her not to say 'Aunt Tamara'.

"I will remember," Kadine said.

"Do you think Uncle Howard will be glad to see us?" Sándor asked.

Judging from the reception so far, Tamara thought, it was rather unlikely, but aloud she said:

"Of course he will, and you must remember that he is Dadda's brother and Dadda would want you to be very nice and polite to him."

"I want Mumma," Vava said. "I do not want to stay here, I want to go home to Mumma!"

Tamara put her arms round the child and drew her close.

Vava was very tired. The journey had been tiring for all of them, but most especially for a child of only five, who wanted to run and jump and not sit cooped up all day in the heat and restriction of a Stage-Coach.

Sometimes they had been fortunate in having it half-empty, but at other times it had been packed and most of the passengers disliked having the windows down, with the result that they felt almost as if they were being suffocated.

"As soon as we have met your uncle," Tamara said to Vava, "I will pop you into bed and bring you a lovely drink. While you are drinking it I will tell you a story."

This promise usually worked like magic, but Vava was too tired to listen.

To make her more comfortable Tamara took off her bonnet, tidied her hair, then held her close in her arms. The child was almost half-asleep when the door opened.

Tamara had expected the Duke to look impressive, but what she had not anticipated was that he should be not only the most magnificent man she had ever seen but also the most handsome.

Lord Ronald had been exceedingly good-looking and the Grant features had been passed to Sándor.

But combined with being over six-foot-three inches tall, broad-shouldered and carrying himself as if he commanded the whole world, the Duke had classical features.

But he had also a cynical and bored look which gave his face an almost sardonic expression.

'He *is* like the villain in my book!' Tamara thought.

Then at the hard look in his eyes as they met hers she felt her heart beat apprehensively as she rose to her feet.

She had thought Lord Ronald looked elegant and smart when he wore evening-clothes, but the Duke dressed for the evening was overwhelming.

Never had she imagined that a man could wear such a dazzlingly white cravat so intricately tied, that his satin evening-coat could fit him as if he were moulded into it, or his knee-breeches and silk stockings give him such a distinguished air.

With an effort she dropped him a low curtsey.

"Who are you and what are you doing here?" the Duke asked.

"You have not received a letter from Mr. Lawson, the Solicitor?"

"A letter?" the Duke queried. "I have heard from no-one, except from the servants who tell me these children are my relatives."

Tamara drew in her breath.

Because the Duke spoke in such a cold, authoritative voice, she felt anger beginning to replace her fear.

"Then Your Grace cannot be aware that your brother Lord Ronald is dead," she replied.

"Dead? Why was I not informed?"

"You should have received a letter telling you of the tragedy two or three days ago."

The Duke was frowning as he came further into the room to walk to the fireplace and stand with his back to it.

"Kindly tell me what happened," he ordered.

"Lord Ronald and his wife were recently drowned at sea, and as there is nowhere else they can go I have brought their children, your nephew and two nieces to you."

Tamara spoke slowly and clearly, her eyes on the Duke's face.

"And who are you?"

"My name is Wynne, Your Grace. I am Governess to the children."

He gave her what she thought was a hostile glance, then he said:

"Surely my brother made some provision for his family?"

"I am afraid not, Your Grace, and as there was nowhere else they could go and they have no money, Mr. Lawson, Lord Ronald's Solicitor, asked me to bring them here to you."

"The devil he did!" the Duke ejaculated. "And what am I supposed to do about them?"

Tamara felt her temper rising.

"I imagine, Your Grace, you will hardly allow them to starve or to be dependent upon charity."

There was a glint in the Duke's eyes as if he resented her tone. Then he turned to look at Sándor who was watching him with curiosity.

"What is your name, boy?"

"Sándor, Uncle Howard."

"How old are you?"

"Nearly twelve."

The Duke looked at Kadine and Tamara thought he must realise how pretty she was with her fair hair and her black-lashed eyes.

Before he could speak Kadine, who was never shy with grown-ups, said:

"You are like my Dadda, only taller. He told me when you were little boys you used to climb to the top of the Castle tower. Can we do that?"

"What is your name?" the Duke enquired.

"Kadine."

"And this is Validé," Tamara said quickly, "only she is always known as Vava which is what she called herself as a baby."

"All extremely theatrical names," the Duke remarked, and Tamara knew he was sneering at her dead sister.

She felt herself quiver with rage but managed to say in a cold, restrained voice:

"As we have travelled for three days, Your Grace, the children are very tired. I think it would be best if I put them to bed and other matters can be discussed later."

"So you intend to stay here," the Duke said.

"Are you suggesting we should go anywhere else?" Tamara enquired.

She thought as she spoke that her hostility was too obvious, but she was hating him as she had expected to do.

She hated his superiority, the way he sneered at the children's names which she felt was a direct insult to her sister, and the manner in which he seemed to be deliberately making them feel uncomfortable and unwanted.

"I suppose there is nothing else to be done to-night, at any rate," he conceded.

"I am tired," Vava wailed suddenly. "I want a drink."

"I am sure that is something, dearest, you will be able to have in a few moments," Tamara answered.

As she spoke she looked at the Duke almost as if she challenged him.

He stared back at her and she thought the lines of cynicism on his face were even more pronounced than when he had first come into the room.

The door opened.

"You rang, Your Grace?"

"Take these children and their Governess to Mrs. Henderson. Inform her that they will be staying in the Castle."

"Yes, Your Grace."

Without saying any more the Duke turned and walked from the room.

Tamara stared after him, wishing there was some way in

which she could hurt him, some way in which she could express the violence of her hatred.

Instead she could do nothing but follow the footman who led them upstairs to the second floor.

Here they waited for some minutes while the Housekeeper was fetched from a different part of the Castle by a maidservant.

When she arrived, obviously annoyed at being disturbed so late in the evening, Tamara saw she was an elderly woman dressed in the rustling black of her calling with a silver chatelaine hanging from her waist.

"Am I right in understanding that you are the Governess to His Grace's nephew and nieces?" she asked Tamara.

"I am," Tamara answered. "My name is Wynne, and I am very glad to meet you, Mrs. Henderson."

The Housekeeper barely touched her fingers.

"It is an extremely inconvenient time of night to arrive and as you were not expected naturally no rooms have been prepared for you."

"The posts must be blamed on that account," Tamara explained. "A letter was sent to His Grace over a week ago."

"From where, may I ask?"

"From Cornwall."

"Oh, Cornwall!"

Mrs. Henderson's intonation of the word could not have been more disparaging had Tamara said it was from hell itself.

"Well, you are here," she said after a moment's pause, "and I suppose I shall have to do something about it. And it must obviously be the Nurseries."

Tamara did not answer but followed the Housekeeper up another long flight of stairs to the third floor of the Castle.

Here were the Nurseries which she realised as they opened the first door, had obviously not been used for many years.

Closed windows had left them smelling stale and airless,

and the fact that the floor had not been brushed or the furniture dusted for some time was very obvious when the candles were lit.

Tamara longed to suggest that there must be other rooms in the Castle that were more habitable, but she thought it really was too late in the evening to enter into any arguments.

The only thing that really mattered was to get Vava to bed for by this time she was almost asleep on her feet.

"I would like some supper for the children, if you please, Mrs. Henderson," Tamara said. "Miss Kadine and Miss Vava usually drink milk, but Master Sándor prefers lemonade."

"I doubt if the Chef has any lemonade ready," Mrs. Henderson replied, "and I cannot imagine what there will be for you to eat."

"Something light, eggs, or soup will do," Tamara said. "I think they are too tired to feel hungry."

"I'll see what can be done," Mrs. Henderson said, "and the house-maids will make up the beds."

She went from the Nursery and Tamara hurried to open the window, then looked around her in dismay.

It must have been years since there had been any painting or decorating on the walls and the furniture was shabby.

She had the feeling that, if once it had been a pleasant, cosy nursery for children, the atmosphere had certainly changed in the years it had lain empty.

The Night-Nurseries were very sparsely furnished, and even when two rather sullen house-maids had made up the beds the rooms seemed to have almost a charity-like austerity.

"I will not be depressed about it," Tamara said to herself. "I am sure by to-morrow things will seem better."

The supper that was finally, after a long wait, brought upstairs did nothing to relieve her depression.

48

It was obvious that nothing could be cooked so late at night. There were some pieces of very dry-looking cold chicken on a plate, half a loaf of bread, a pat of butter, a jug of milk and one of water.

The servant who brought it plonked it on its tray down on a table and disappeared before Tamara could ask for a tablecloth.

Vava was far too tired even to want the milk. Tamara put her straight into bed and she was asleep as her head touched the pillow.

"This is a jolly rotten supper," Sándor remarked.

Tamara agreed with him, but thought it best not to say so.

"They were not expecting us and we are causing a lot of work late at night, so we cannot be particular."

"There is no salt," Sándor said.

"Never mind," Tamara answered. "This is just a picnic and people always forget things on a picnic."

Kadine was too tired to fancy cold chicken, but Tamara managed to persuade her to eat a very thin slice of bread and butter and drink some milk. Then she too went to bed.

"My room is much smaller than the one I had at home," Sándor said. "I expected to have a big room in such a huge Castle."

"We will see if we can find you a better one to-morrow," Tamara answered.

"Shall I ask Uncle Howard if I can ride his horses?" Sándor enquired.

"We will ask him at the first opportunity," Tamara promised.

But she could not help thinking that if this was a sample of the hospitality they were to receive at the Castle any concession might be hard to obtain.

But there was no point in arguing about things to-night, and when their luggage was brought up by the footmen she took out only the night clothes they needed, deciding to leave

49

all the rest of the unpacking until the following day.

She too was tired, but when she got into bed she found it difficult to sleep.

Instead she lay awake hating the Duke, and yet at the same time acknowledging that he was without exception the most impressive man she had ever seen in her life.

'He is just as a Duke should look,' she thought, and the description of him in her novel was rather apt.

The fictitious Duke had been called Ullester, and although his villainy had projected itself in the expression on his face he used his physical attractions like his rank, to further his nefarious ends.

'I wish Mr. Lawson had not made me withdraw the book from publication,' Tamara thought. 'I am quite certain that this Duke would not read novels and if he did, he would be far too conceited to recognise himself.'

Yet from what she had seen already of the Castle, her descriptions had been surprisingly accurate and combined with the servants' liveries and other details in the tale, there was an uncomfortable resemblance to the truth.

The hero, the Duke's brother, Lord Tristan, was every-thing a hero should be – kind, generous, big-hearted, a champion of the down-trodden and a protector of the poor.

When he wished to marry the entrancingly lovely heroine with a face like an angel, the wicked Duke had forbidden the marriage and threatened all sorts of dreadful vengeance and penalties if his brother should disobey his command.

What was more, he persecuted the heroine's family, turn-ing her father out of his house with the result that her mother died of privation and her sisters and brothers came to the verge of starvation.

Needless to say, the Duke's accidental death and his brother's inheritance of the title brought the novel to a happy conclusion.

"I will change the descriptions of the Castle and the

liveries," Tamara decided. "I can make the Duke the hero's cousin rather than his brother, then I can publish the book, with a different title."

It was a pity because she thought 'The Ducal Wasp' was an amusing and provocative name.

At the same time, if the children had to live under his roof it would be a mistake for the Duke to be made more incensed than he was already.

It was long after midnight before finally she ceased thinking of the changes she could make to her novel.

She fell asleep, only to dream that the Duke of Granchester was tearing the pages from her book and throwing them out from the tower up which they were all climbing to reach him.

"I hate you . . . I hate you . . ." Tamara was calling out in her dream.

CHAPTER THREE

Tamara awoke with a start and jumped out of bed.

She pulled back the curtains and as the sunlight flooded in she told herself that to-day would be better. Things would be brighter both for herself and the children.

The Nurseries looked out at the back of the Castle and she could see flower-gardens which were a kaleidoscope of colour, walls of Tudor red brick and woods which rose dark green and mysterious to the skyline.

It was very beautiful and Tamara felt her spirits rise.

'There will be lots of places to explore and the children will love that,' she thought to herself. 'I will ask the Duke if they can ride, and perhaps I can go with them.'

Her eyes shone at the thought of riding really fine horses.

There had been friends of her father's at Oxford who had often allowed her to exercise their horses in the summer when they were unable to hunt.

She knew that she rode well and that if she had a choice she would rather ride than take any other form of exercise.

But she had the uncomfortable feeling that the Duke would perhaps expect his grooms to accompany the children and she would be left behind.

"I will explain," she told herself, "that I have been giving Vava lessons; then surely he will not refuse me?"

With a little grimace she told herself that the Duke could do anything he wished to do, and it was doubtful if anyone could persuade him to agree to anything that did not concur with his own selfish interests.

Determined not to let anything depress her, Tamara dressed then woke the children.

Sándor was up already and when she appeared he asked:

"May I go downstairs and explore before breakfast, Aunt Tama . . . I mean Miss Wynne? I can see some deer under the trees in the Park and I want to get a closer look at them."

"Yes, of course, you may," Tamara agreed, "but do not be late for breakfast. I expect they will bring it up at about half-past-eight."

But that, unfortunately, was wishful thinking.

At ten-minutes-to-nine Tamara rang the bell and when a housemaid appeared she asked if they could have their breakfast.

"Breakfast, Miss?" the housemaid repeated as if it was a meal she had never heard of. "I don't think Mrs. Henderson gave orders for any to be brought upstairs."

"Well, we can go downstairs, if that is more convenient," Tamara answered, "but we would like it as soon as possible. We are all rather hungry after such a small supper last night."

The maid disappeared and it was nearly half-an-hour later before she came back with a tray.

She set it down on the table with a thump and looked surprised when Tamara asked her to fetch a table-cloth.

On a dish which was uncovered there were four poached eggs which were already cold, reposing on some plain untoasted pieces of bread. There was also a loaf of bread on the tray, butter and a pot of plum jam, which all the children disliked.

There was a large pot of very strong tea and a small jug of milk.

The plates for the eggs had, Tamara felt sure, never been heated and once again there was no salt or pepper and only three cups and saucers.

She asked the maid to fetch some more milk, another cup and salt.

It was so long in coming that when it did arrive the children had eaten what they could of the very unappetising breakfast and were longing to go out into the sunshine.

"I do not like my egg cold," Vava said fretfully.

"Nor do any of us," Tamara agreed. "I will speak to Mrs. Henderson and see if something better cannot be arranged for to-morrow morning."

She felt, however it was important for her first to see the Duke.

She felt there would be many questions he would wish to ask regarding his brother and even more about the children, but she was not sent for.

When she finally enquired of a footman whether the Duke wished to see her she was informed that he had gone out early in the morning and would not be back until just before dinner.

This at least left them free to explore the gardens and the stables where Sándor went into ecstasies over the horses and Vava begged to be lifted up onto one.

The Head Groom, who seemed to be the only pleasant servant they had met so far, answered Vava's pleadings by leading her around the stable-yard on a horse that was just going out for exercise.

When Tamara explained that they were Lord Ronald's children he became very interested in them.

"Oi remembers Lord Ronald – a fine rider His Lordship were," he said. "Fearless, and would ride anythin' however wild. Oi can see the young gentleman has the very look of him."

"I would like to have the chance to show that I can ride as well as my father," Sándor said.

"Ye must talk to 'is Grace, young Sir," the groom replied,

"and p'raps he'll be buying a pony for th' young ladies."

He looked at Tamara enquiringly as he spoke and she smiled.

"We are hoping that," she answered, "and I think you will find that Miss Vava is also as fearless as Lord Ronald."

Vava in fact disgraced herself by screaming and yelling when she was taken down from the horse's back.

"I want to go riding!" she kept crying.

Only the suggestion that they would go and look for fish in the lake prevented her from running after the grooms when they set out to exercise the horses.

"I wish I could go with them," Sándor said wistfully.

"We must ask your uncle first," Tamara replied.

There was so much to see however that the children enjoyed every moment of the morning until they went back to the Castle for luncheon.

Tamara had asked to see Mrs. Henderson before they went out, but was told she was busy. When she asked for her now the Housekeeper came up to the Nursery with what Tamara knew was an unco-operative expression on her face.

"I am afraid there was not enough breakfast for the children," Tamara said, "and as the eggs were left uncovered they were quite cold by the time they reached here."

"That's not my business, Miss Wynne," Mrs. Henderson replied coldly. "I told the Chef you required breakfast, as I've told him you'll require luncheon. The menus are left to him as His Grace entrusts him with the food that's required for the Dining-Room."

"I do appreciate that it is a long way for everything to be brought," Tamara said, "but surely there are other rooms in the Castle which are more accessible?"

"There are many rooms in the Castle, Miss Wynne," Mrs. Henderson replied, "but they are certainly not suitable for children!"

"I think you will find that these children are not destructive in any way," Tamara said.

She gave the Housekeeper what she hoped was an ingratiating smile as she went on:

"They have been so much with their parents and in fact always used the best rooms at home, so they appreciate fine things and can be trusted with them."

It was true, she thought, that Lord Ronald and his wife had loved their children so much that only the best was good enough for them.

At the Manor the children had occupied the bed-rooms which other people would have kept for guests, and when they were not with their parents they had what was called 'The Nursery'.

This was on the ground floor and one of the most charming and well-furnished Sitting-rooms in the whole house.

Mrs. Henderson, as though she had nothing more to say was moving away when Tamara said:

"Will the housemaids be coming up to clean these rooms to-day? I am sure you will appreciate that having been shut up for so long they are somewhat dusty."

"I am afraid my girls are too busy," Mrs. Henderson replied. "Perhaps later in the week they may have an hour or two to spare, but for the moment I cannot promise you any assistance, Miss Wynne, in keeping these rooms clean."

She stalked away and Tamara knew that she was resenting the children simply because it meant extra work and the disruption of what she was quite sure was a lazy way of life.

"It is what might be expected of the servants of a man like the Duke," she told herself angrily.

She went back to the Nursery to make their beds while waiting for luncheon which was again over half-an-hour late.

This time it was quite inedible. There was a piece of mutton that was so badly cooked that the children could not get their teeth into it and it was again cold when it reached them.

There were no vegetables, only a dish of over-cooked potatoes, and half a heavy and unappetising suet pudding with no custard or treacle to go with it.

The food at the Manor had always been plain but extremely well cooked either by Maïka or Tamara, or by Lucy, whom they had taught to be nearly as good a cook as they were themselves.

Because Maïka could not bear her husband to suffer in any way because he had married her she would devise for him the most delicious continental dishes which she had been taught by her mother.

In the evening the three of them used to eat meals that Lord Ronald said were unequalled by anything he had ever tasted before.

While it was not good for the children to have the rich sauces which their father enjoyed, everything they ate was not only beneficial but also delicious.

Lord Ronald would grow special vegetables and fruit in the garden which they had learnt to appreciate and Tamara knew that not only would they miss these but their absence must affect their health.

"I cannot eat this," Sándor said after he had struggled manfully to cut up the mutton and failed.

"Nor can I," Tamara said helplessly.

"I am hungry!" Vava wailed. "I am hungry!"

"I will see your uncle and maybe everything will be better to-morrow," Tamara promised.

She thought as she spoke it was not going to be easy and she had the feeling that the Duke's attitude towards them of indifference and lack of attention was only being echoed by his servants.

"Let's go into the garden and pick some peaches," Sándor suggested as he pushed aside the suet pudding. "I saw dozens of them when I was exploring this morning."

Although Tamara thought perhaps that would be a mistake, the mere fact that his suggestion cheered up Kadine and Vava made her agree somewhat weakly to follow him into the kitchen-garden.

She expected they would find a gardener there whom she could ask if they could have some fruit, but there seemed to be no-one about and Sándor disappeared into the peach-house.

He came back with four huge peaches, all ripe and so juicy and delicious that Tamara forgot her scruples and enjoyed them as much as the children.

In another house they found grapes, huge purple muscats, and they cut off a bunch and ate them.

Then wandering round the garden they discovered green-gages and nectarines, and rows of raspberries in a cage made of netting so that the birds could not get at them.

"We shall all have tummy-aches if we eat any more fruit," Tamara warned. "Suppose we pick the raspberries and take them back for supper?"

"Let us ask for some cream to go with them," Kadine cried. "You know how Dadda always said raspberries and cream were his favourite fruit."

"Mumma liked peaches best," Sándor said.

"I want another peach," Vava said greedily, but Tamara said firmly that she had had enough.

She noted however as they walked back through the garden that there were plenty of peas ready to pick and every other sort of vegetable, including crisp lettuces.

"Cut one of those," she told Sándor, "and if nothing nice is sent up for tea I will make you some lettuce sandwiches."

The children liked these and Sándor cut two lettuces with his pen-knife. They also pulled some radishes which they found in another neat row to take back to the house.

It was certainly not a very substantial meal, but at least it was better than feeling the pangs of hunger, and when tea-time came and, as Tamara had expected, the only thing that was brought upstairs was the inevitable loaf of bread, and plum jam, she made the children lettuce sandwiches.

They ate the radishes with them and although they missed the dainty cakes, the scones and all the other delicacies they would have enjoyed at home, they did not complain.

The raspberries, which had made a considerable mess of Sándor's cap, Tamara was keeping for supper.

By this time she was feeling very hungry herself and when the meal came up it was again pieces of cold chicken, although this time there were four thickly cut slices of ham.

There was however a big jug of milk and she made Vava bread and milk and persuaded her with some difficulty to eat a little of the chicken which she cut up very small.

Although she had asked for cream they received none and had to make do with raspberries and milk, which was however, better than nothing.

"I will speak to the Duke to-night and tell him this cannot go on," Tamara told herself.

When Vava and Kadine were in bed she went down to the Hall to ask if the Duke would see her. She was however informed that His Grace had gone out to dinner, leaving early as he had some distance to drive.

The fact that he had come back to the house and made no effort to see her or the children was infuriating, but there was nothing Tamara could do about it.

She asked if the Duke would see her without fail to-morrow morning, as it was of importance.

"I'll give His Grace your message, Miss," the Butler said in a voice which showed her all too clearly that he thought her insistence was an impertinence.

She went back upstairs and after the children had gone to bed tried to read one of her favourite books which she had brought with her in the luggage.

But she found it impossible to do anything but think of the uncomfortable position they were in, the way they were being treated at the Castle, and the fact that the Duke obviously intended to ignore them.

"If this goes on, what am I to do?" she wondered.

She asked herself the same question the following morning when, after waiting to hear from the Duke, she went downstairs at ten o'clock to be informed that His Grace had once again left the Castle early and the servants had no idea when he would return.

"Is there no-one else with any authority to whom I can speak?" she asked the Butler, with a peremptory note in her voice which made him look at her in surprise.

"His Grace's comptroller is in London at the moment," the Butler replied. "We are expecting Major Melville to return at the beginning of next week. I am sure then, Miss, he will deal with any enquiries you may wish to make."

"The beginning of next week!" Tamara exclaimed.

That was four days ahead and she had the feeling that by that time they would all be hungry and the children's health might well suffer for lack of proper food.

They went out during the morning, but Tamara was very quiet. She was thinking what she could do.

When once again a quite inedible meal was sent up at luncheon-time she looked at it, then told all three children to follow her.

"Where are we going?" Sándor asked.

"You will see," Tamara answered grimly.

She knew where the back stairs were by this time, and they went down to find themselves as she expected on reaching the ground floor, in the kitchen quarters.

She walked resolutely along the flagged passage until she came to the big high-ceilinged kitchen where there was a Chef and a number of scullions grouped found a huge stove.

They were cooking, she thought, a meal for the staff and it certainly smelt better than the food that had been sent upstairs.

"Good-morning!" she said to the Chef.

He turned to look at her and stared with surprise at the three children who followed her.

"*Bonjour!*" he said after a moment.

"*Bonjour, Monsieur!*" Tamara replied in French, then continued: "We have come, *Monsieur*, to see you, because I cannot imagine the food that is being brought upstairs for His Grace's nephew and nieces can have been sent by you."

The Chef looked surprised, then he replied truculently:

"What is wrong with it?"

"You can hardly expect me to explain to a Frenchman what is wrong with food which is inedible," Tamara replied.

Her answer stung him into a retaliation and he burst into a flood of volubility, saying that it was not his job to cook for Nurseries and he had not enough help in the kitchen except to provide meals for His Grace and his friends, and for the present staff.

Tamara waited while he talked himself to a standstill, then said:

"If you have not enough help then I will cook a meal for these children; for I do not intend them to become ill from eating food which could only be intended for pigs."

Her words were ruder in French than in English and, as she had intended, the Frenchman was infuriated by her insult.

He worked himself to a frenzy, gesticulating in almost incoherent rage, and ending:

"As I said, I have not enough help and you either eat what I send you or go without!"

"I have no intention of doing either of those things," Tamara replied. "As we are very hungry, I intend now to cook a meal for my charges for they can no longer go without proper food."

She walked resolutely to the kitchen-table as she spoke and the Frenchman throwing up his arms shouted furiously:

"Do as you like! I will leave! I will not be insulted in my own kitchen!"

He walked away towards the door as he spoke and Tamara looking at the open-mouthed scullions said in English:

"Bring me a clean pan, eggs, butter, salt, pepper and a basin."

They looked at her in astonishment, then because her voice was firm and she had an air of authority about her they obeyed.

"Please put a cloth on that table and lay it for four," and to the children she said: "Sit down, darlings, and you will have some decent food as soon as I have cooked it for you."

She put a large lump of butter into the pan and set it on the stove to melt. As she did so she saw there were several chickens on a spit and she told one of the scullions to start turning it.

As he did so she first threw some salt and pepper on the nearest chicken, then broke a dozen eggs into a basin, stirring them with a fork while the butter was melting in the pan.

There were some tomatoes on a sideboard. She told a scullion to put six into hot water, then peel them and remove the seeds.

Just before she poured the eggs into the pan she told the boy who had been preparing the tomatoes to put them in another pan with a little butter.

She folded these into the omelette at the last moment and then she turned it over onto a hot dish which a scullion had taken from the oven with four plates. It was moist at the centre and perfectly rounded and golden brown on the top.

She carried it to the table and set it down in front of the children.

"Help yourselves, darlings," she said. "I will see to the chicken."

She threw more salt and pepper on it and now it was

beginning to smell delicious as it turned and turned in front of the hot fire.

She set some small mushrooms to simmer on the stove and asked the scullions for a wooden bowl, but that was not procurable.

When they brought her a glass one, lettuces and a knife, she told them knives should never be used on a green salad'

"You must pull off the leaves gently with your fingers," she instructed, "then toss them in the dressing."

She made the dressing, which was the one the children liked with oil, vinegar, mustard and a little sugar.

By this time the chicken was ready and she carved it deftly, jointing it in a foreign fashion, garnished it with watercress and small mushrooms which she had set in another pan to cook.

There was only a small piece of the omelette left for her when she sat down for a moment at the table. The children told her how much they had enjoyed it and were now waiting eagerly for the chicken.

She gave the white meat to Kadine and Vava while she and Sándor enjoyed the darker portions.

It was delicious with the fresh salad and the little button mushrooms which had been cooked exactly right.

Tamara ate quickly, then she rose from the table to ask if there was any fruit.

The scullions said there were raspberries and red currants and she told them to bring her the latter together with the white of egg and icing sugar.

They looked at her in surprise and watched with interest as she held a string of red currants between her thumb and first finger, dipped it in the white of egg, let it drip, then rolled it in the icing sugar.

It was a dish the children loved and a whole plateful of white-sugared currants quickly disappeared. Vava said grace and they rose from the table.

"Thank you for all your help," Tamara said to the scullions. "It would be a great kindness if you would bake us a cake and some scones for tea."

They smiled at her encouragingly and she looked towards the Chef who was still standing just inside the kitchen watching her as he had done all the while she was cooking.

"I must thank you, *Monsieur*," she said in French, "for your hospitality. It is the first decent meal we have eaten since we came to stay with His Grace, and I am hoping it will not be the last!"

In response the Frenchman made a sound which was one of mingled fury and derision, then he said:

"I resign! I will not stay here and be insulted, then we shall see what matters most to His Grace – a lot of tiresome brats, or his food!"

With that he stormed out of the kitchen and Tamara looked at the children.

"We have caused a storm," she said, "and I have a feeling there is even rougher weather ahead."

The two little girls did not understand, but Sándor laughed.

"You are very brave," he said, "but I think Mumma would have done the same thing."

"I am quite certain she would!" Tamara answered. "And that is why, Sándor, we are, none of us, going to be afraid!"

Kadine and Vava lay down after luncheon and Tamara helped Sándor to study one of his Latin books.

In Cornwall he had been taught by the Vicar, although in fact Tamara was extremely proficient in Latin.

"What is going to happen about my lessons?" Sándor asked.

"The inevitable answer is that we have to wait until I have seen the Duke," Tamara smiled, "but I am sure there is a big Library somewhere in this building. I can remember your father telling me about it."

"Let us go down and see the Librarian, if there is one," Sándor suggested.

They found an old man in what Tamara thought was one of the most magnificent Libraries she had ever seen.

He told them that his name was Aitken and he was the Curator of the whole Castle.

Sándor immediately bombarded him with questions about the Norman Keep, the dungeons and a dozen other things that particularly interested him.

Mr. Aitken remembered Lord Ronald well and told them that as far as he was concerned they were welcome to take any book they required from the Library.

Tamara felt excited to know how much reading she could do and how many volumes there were that would be of particular interest not only to her but also to Sándor.

They could not stay long because she did not like to leave the little girls and when Kadine and Vava rose after their rest they all went on Sándor's insistence back to the stables.

Because luncheon had been so delayed it was getting late in the afternoon but Abbey, the old groom, was pleased to see them and once again allowed Vava to sit on the saddle of one of the horses.

"Do you train a lot of race horses here?" Sándor asked eagerly.

"A great many, young Master," the groom replied, "and His Grace is running two o' them at Cheltenham Races this week. Wer're a-hoping one will win th' Steeple-Chase Cup."

'The Cheltenham Races,' Tamara thought to herself.

So that was where the Duke had been these past days, and there was perhaps some excuse for his leaving the problem of the children until after the race-meeting.

At the same time he might, she thought, have sent them a message to inform them why he was so busy.

"How do you train the horses?" Sándor was asking.

The old groom chuckled.

65

"Oi'll show ye, young Sir."

He took them the whole length of the stables to where at the far end they saw in an open field a miniature race-course.

Tamara remembered that Lord Ronald had once said there was such a thing in the Castle grounds and she had incorporated it in her novel.

It was therefore somewhat uncanny to see the huge jumps just as she had described them.

"They look quite easy," Sándor said after inspecting the course for some time.

The old groom laughed.

"Ye'd not be saying that if ye were a-riding, Master Sándor. There'll be many a horse falling at Cheltenham this week over exactly th' same jumps as ye see here."

Sándor said nothing but he went on looking at the artificial hedges and wide water-jump. Then he noticed that not on the race-course but at the side of it there was a five-bar gate.

"Do you train the horses over that, too?" he enquired.

"That's His Grace's new jump which he keeps exclusively for himself," the groom replied. "It's not for th' racing horses but for th' hunters."

"It is a good idea," Sándor said enthusiastically.

"His Grace has had it set up in th' new manner," the groom explained. "If the horse he's training doesn't clear the top bar th' gate falls."

"That saves a lot of broken knees," Sándor laughed.

He ran up to the gate and inspected it and saw that, as the groom had said, it was only lightly attached to two posts on either side.

A horse striking the top bar with his hoofs would simply knock the gate down and would therefore not be in danger of falling himself.

Tamara heard Vava calling to her and went to the child's side.

"I want to go faster, much faster!" Vava was saying to the young groom who was leading her.

"You are going fast enough," Tamara smiled. "This is a much bigger pony than you rode at home."

"I want to gallop," Vava said obstinately.

"Her's got a sporting instinct in her, like her brother," the old groom said beside her.

Tamara looked round to see that somehow Sándor had persuaded the old man in her absence to let him mount one of the horses which had just come into the yard after being exercised.

It was a large black stallion and as the young groom swung himself down from the saddle he had said:

"Samson's fair pulled me arms out o' me sockets. But Oi've ridden him hard an' some o' th' devil's gone out o' him."

"That's good," the Head Groom approved.

Sándor was riding down the yard obviously delighted at being mounted on such a fine horse.

"He is magnificent, is he not, Miss Wynne?" he called.

"And very much larger than Rufus," she replied.

Sándor turned the stallion's head and rode a little faster to the end of the cobbled yard, then as if he suddenly made up his mind he took the stallion onto the race-course.

The old groom started forward with a cry.

"Come back, young Sir, ye're not to go a-jumping that horse. He be too big for ye."

But either Sándor did not hear him or had no intention of doing so, for he started to ride round the course, taking the first jump in fine style and going on to the next.

"It's not right, if the young gentleman has a fall His Grace'll be a-blaming me," old Abbey muttered.

"You need not worry," Tamara said calmly. "Master Sándor is a very good rider and although he has never been on anything so magnificent as that animal he has in fact ridden a number of different horses over the years."

Sándor cleared another fence and now he was going to the water-jump.

Watching him, Tamara realised the boy was using all his intelligence. He was approaching each fence under control and at exactly the right moment lifted the stallion in a manner which made the horse sail over the obstacles in a way which might have been expected of any professional rider.

Because she was so pleased with what he had achieved she gave a little cry and clapped her hands together.

"Good! That is very good!" she exclaimed. "I knew he could do it!"

Then a voice behind her asked harshly:

"May I enquire what is going on here?"

With a leap of her heart Tamara realised that while they were watching Sándor, the Duke had approached them from the yard and they had not heard him.

She and the groom turned round hastily.

The Duke was looking even more magnificent and authoritative than before in champagne-coloured pantaloons and brilliantly polished Hessians.

He had a high hat on the side of his dark head and with him was another gentleman, older than he was, but also arrayed in the height of fashion.

The latter was looking at Tamara through a quizzing glass which made her suddenly conscious of her appearance.

She had not expected the Duke until later and as it was very hot she had put on one of her thin muslin gowns and wore her hair in a less formal style than the way she had arranged it when they first arrived.

Because she was only with the children she had taken off her bonnet which was dangling from her arm by its ribbons.

Without seeing the criticism in the Duke's eyes, she knew she was not behaving with the propriety that he might have expected of a Governess.

She curtsied and looked apprehensively at him to see that he was watching Sándor.

"Who allowed that boy to ride my horse?" he asked.

"Oi lets him just mount Samson in the yard, Your Grace," the Head Groom said apologetically, "but the young gentleman takes him onto the race-course afore Oi could stop him."

Sándor cleared another fence and the old man added:

"Th' spit and image of his father, he be! He'll be as good a rider as Your Grace in a few years."

The Duke's lips tightened in what Tamara thought was an ominous manner then the gentleman beside him said with a laugh:

"I was not aware, Howard, that you had children at the Castle, but will you not introduce me to the very charming young lady who apparently is in charge of them?"

"This is their Governess," the Duke said in an uncompromising tone.

"I should still like to meet her," his friend insisted.

To avoid further embarrassment Tamara turned away to go to Vava who was still being led around the yard.

"It is time to go back for tea," she said.

"I want to go on riding," Vava replied almost fiercely, "I want to go faster."

"I want my tea," Kadine said.

She had been feeding the horses in the stalls with pieces of carrot which one of the stable-boys handed to her.

"We will go in as soon as Sándor has finished riding," Tamara said.

Kadine looked in the direction of the race-course and saw the Duke.

"There is Uncle Howard," she exclaimed. "I am going to ask him if he will give me a pony."

She ran up the yard before Tamara could stop her and,

quite unabashed by the Duke, slipped her hand into his.

He looked down at her with astonishment as she said:

"Please Uncle Howard, may I have a pony? I had one at home and I want to ride like Sándor, but I would like a pony of my own."

Her face was turned pleadingly up to his and the Duke's friend laughed.

"If you can refuse a request put so prettily, Howard, I shall be astonished."

He dropped his quizzing glass and picked Kadine up in his arms.

"What is your name, little lady?"

"Kadine," she answered, "what is yours?"

"My name is Cropthorne."

"That is a funny name!"

"Do you think so? Your name is very pretty. As pretty as you are."

"I am not as pretty as my Mumma."

"Then she must be very pretty indeed."

Kadine suddenly struggled in his arms.

"I want to go and have my tea," she said. "It was horrid yesterday, but I think we will have a cake to-day."

She was put down on the ground. The gentleman took hold of her hand and walked back to Tamara.

"I hear you are having cake for tea," he said. "Am I invited to join you?"

There was something in the way he spoke and the look in his eyes which made Tamara feel he was dangerous.

"I hardly think you will enjoy nursery tea, Sir," she replied.

"It is certainly a long time since I partook of one," he answered, "but I would enjoy anything, if it was in your company."

There was no mistaking the flirtatious note in his voice or the way he was looking at her, and the colour rose in

Tamara's face as she helped a protesting Vava down from the saddle.

As she did so, she realised that Sándor had finished the course and was bringing the stallion back to the stables.

His cheeks were flushed with excitement, his eyes shining and when he saw the Duke he cried out:

"This is a wonderful horse, Uncle Howard! Please, may I ride him again?"

"You did not have my permission this time," the Duke said severely.

"Miss Wynne was going to ask you this morning," Sándor answered, "but you had gone out, and I did want to try out your jumps."

"Ye' shouldn't have gone over them without asking Oi first," the Head Groom said. "Ye might have had a fall, young Sir, and ye'd have got me into trouble."

"I have had lots of falls," Sándor boasted. "My father always made me get on again immediately, so I am not afraid."

He sprang down from the stallion's back and walked to the Duke's side.

"You will let me ride your horses, Uncle Howard, will you not?" he begged.

"It depends on a great number of things," the Duke replied coldly. "I will discuss the matter with your Governess when I have the time."

He walked away as he spoke leaving Sándor staring after him.

He passed Tamara who was holding Vava by the hand and walked with immense dignity and presence back towards the Castle.

His friend followed him but paused to say to Tamara in a low voice:

"Even if I am not invited to tea we shall meet again, fair Enchantress, I will make sure of that!"

71

Tamara did not reply, but he smiled at her in what she felt was a far too familiar manner before he followed the Duke down the yard.

"Do you think Uncle Howard means to let me ride?" Sándor asked.

"I hope so," Tamara answered, "but he is certainly very unpredictable. It is unfortunate that he returned from the races far earlier than we expected."

Because she did not wish the children to be oppressed by her feelings she said brightly:

"Thank Abbey for letting you ride, Sándor, and now we will all run back as quickly as we can to have our tea."

They went upstairs to the Nursery to find the scullions had not failed Tamara's request: there was a cake and scones for their tea besides a comb of honey and a pot of home-made strawberry jam.

"Things are getting better," Tamara said brightly.

But she could not help wondering whether they were getting worse where the Duke was concerned.

He certainly did not seem proud of his nephew's riding ability, but rather the opposite, and she had a feeling that his friend's compliments would make her position in the Duke's eyes even more difficult than it was already.

She had a sudden longing to escape.

If only they could go back to Cornwall, if only they had not been obliged to leave the quiet happiness of the Manor.

Once again she felt she was being over-powered by the Castle, the hostile servants and most of all by the Duke!

"I hate him," she said again to herself as if it was a talisman to give her courage!

CHAPTER FOUR

Tamara anticipated that the Duke would send for her later in the day, so she changed into her green gown and re-arranged her hair, pinning it into a bun at the back of her head as it had been on her arrival.

She could not help feeling that the severity of the style seemed to make the size and darkness of her eyes even more prominent.

But she hoped that the Duke would notice her as little as possible and, more important than anything else, think she looked older than she was.

The summons came at six o'clock, just as she was putting Vava into bed. A footman came to the Nursery door.

"His Grace wishes to see you, Miss."

"If you will wait two minutes," Tamara answered, "you can take me to His Grace."

"He's in the Blue Salon, Miss."

"As I have no idea where that is I should be grateful if you would wait for me."

The footman acquiesced, but leant somewhat familiarly against the jamb of the door thinking, Tamara knew, that as she was only a servant like himself, there was no need to be particularly respectful.

She carried Vava to the Night-Nursery and put her to bed, then made Kadine promise that when she had finished her milk she would go to her own room.

"Look after them, Sándor," she begged.

He was sitting reading by the window and he answered:

"All right, but do not forget to ask if I can ride all the horses in the stables."

"You will be lucky if you get permission to ride one," Tamara answered, "but I will do my best."

She took a last glance at herself in the mirror, smoothing her hair down at the side of her forehead where a few tendrils had escaped when Vava had flung her arms around her neck.

She told herself it was absurd to be frightened.

Yet she knew as she followed the footman down the stairs and through the great Hall that she was nervous as she had never felt nervous of any other person in her whole life.

'It is not because I am afraid of him personally,' she thought, 'but because he may try to prevent me from looking after the children.'

The footman opened a door.

"Miss Wynne, Your Grace!" he said and Tamara walked into the room.

The Duke was alone, standing at the far end of the Salon with his back to the fireplace.

Because it was summer there was no fire and she thought that he made the hearth-rug seem almost a dais from which he reigned supreme and she was nothing but a suppliant coming before him almost on her knees.

He was looking extremely handsome, she admitted, but the lines of cynicism were very pronounced and his expression looked like one of contempt.

Even before he spoke she resented his attitude, her chin went up and there was a defiant look in her eyes, that she could not suppress as she came nearer to him.

She curtsied and stood waiting; she felt he was looking her over in a searching fashion which made her temper begin to rise.

74

"You seem to have taken a great many liberties since you arrived in my house," the Duke said at length.

Tamara did not speak and he went on:

"I have been informed that the children, who are obviously out of hand, have been stealing fruit from the greenhouses and that you and they have caused a commotion in the kitchen, to such an extent that my Chef has threatened to leave."

Tamara could not help feeling slightly amused.

She had been quite certain that the Chef would not actually hand in his notice as he had said he would. He would merely make trouble.

"Well, what have you to say for yourself?" the Duke asked.

"A great deal, Your Grace," Tamara answered coolly. "First I am not prepared to stand by and watch the children starve or be made ill by eating unsuitable food, and I should not have thought that the picking of fruit in their uncle's garden would come in the category of stealing."

"What is wrong with the food?" the Duke asked.

"It is both insufficient and inedible!"

"In your opinion?"

"In anyone's opinion. The children were able to eat practically nothing yesterday and were therefore so hungry that I was forced to cook them a decent meal myself, the first they have had since they entered the Castle."

"I can hardly credit that my Chef, whose cooking has been acclaimed by a great many connoisseurs, is not good enough for three children and yourself, Miss Wynne."

"It is hardly a question of cooking," Tamara answered. "The eggs that were sent up for breakfast were cold before they reached the top floor. The left-over pieces of cold chicken and mutton that were too tough to be eaten in the Servants' Hall were considered to be good enough for children in whom Your Grace obviously has no interest."

She thought he was about to speak and went on quickly:

"Servants ape their masters, and the fact that you have not welcomed your brother's children is of course reflected in the way they are treated not only by the kitchen staff but also by everyone else in the household."

She raised her chin a little higher as she added:

"In case Your Grace is not aware of it, it is not the place of a Governess who is employed to teach and to take general charge to have to make beds and clean floors because there are no housemaids available to perform these tasks."

"You surprise me, Miss Wynne," the Duke said slowly.

"I have something to suggest to Your Grace."

"What is it?" he enquired.

"If you will give me the same allowance for the children that you gave your brother, I will take them away from here, back to Cornwall. The house in which they lived there would be too big and anyway it is sold, but I should be able to find another house we could afford."

"I have never heard such a preposterous suggestion in the whole of my life!" the Duke said sharply. "It is not your place, Miss Wynne, to be the Guardian of these children, nor are you old enough to act in such a capacity."

Tamara did not speak but she made a little gesture with her hands. The Duke said:

"I received yesterday the letter from my brother's Solicitors in Cornwall telling me what had occurred and informing me that you and the children were arriving here. The letter had been delayed en route owing, I understand, to an accident to the Mail Coach which was carrying it."

"It was unfortunate that we arrived first," Tamara said.

"Very," the Duke agreed. "But now you are here, I presume I must make arrangements that you, Miss Wynne, will consider suitable."

He was being sarcastic, and there was a note in his voice that made her feel as if he flicked her with a whip.

"And the first thing I would ask Your Grace," she said, "is that Sándor, who is nearly twelve, should go to school."

"He has been well taught?"

"I think you will find he is well in advance of most boys of his age."

"And you have been his teacher?"

There was a mocking twist to the Duke's lips which she did not miss.

"I have taught Sándor languages," she replied. "He speaks fluent French and good Italian, and he has learnt Latin with our Vicar, who is a classical scholar."

"Is that all?"

"I have taught him Arithmetic, Geography and English Literature, Your Grace."

"And yet you do not look English."

"My father was English."

"And your mother?"

"Hungarian."

"Which of course accounts for the colour of your hair."

Tamara did not answer. She merely raised her eye-brows.

"Well, let us hope," he said after a moment's pause, "that my nephew will not be unmercifully ragged at school for having such a fanciful, or as I said before, theatrical name."

"Your Grace's knowledge is lamentably at fault," Tamara replied. "Sándor is not a theatrical name. It is the name of one of the oldest and most respected families in Hungary. Count Andressy Sandor was in fact a National hero, and most students of history have heard of him."

She had meant to score off the Duke and she succeeded, for she saw the surprise on his face and added before he could speak:

"Actually Count Andressy Sandor was Lady Ronald's grandfather!"

"She was Hungarian!" the Duke exclaimed. "I had no idea."

Then almost to himself, as if he could not let the opportunity pass he added:

"But she was an actress."

"She was nothing of the sort!" Tamara said sharply. "Lady Ronald was a singer. She had an exceptionally fine voice and she sang for two years with a private Opera Company because her mother had had a long illness and the bills could not have been paid otherwise."

She saw the Duke raise his eyebrows in surprise and continued:

"The Opera Company has recently come under the patronage of the Countess of Rockingham who could tell you more about it if Your Grace is interested."

The Duke was obviously startled.

"The Countess of Rockingham? But she is a relative of mine," he said. "I have heard of this Opera Company she sponsors, in fact I believe I have subscribed to it."

"Then you will understand that Lady Ronald was not an actress in the usually accepted meaning of the word."

"You certainly know more about her than I do, Miss Wynne."

There was an unmistakable note of sincerity in his voice and Tamara said in a different tone:

"I not only acted as Governess to Lady Ronald's children, I had also the privilege of being her . . . friend."

"Because you were both Hungarian."

"I have already said, Your Grace, that my father was English."

"And do you really believe that being somewhat of a foreigner you are capable of teaching English Literature to my nieces, and apparently also to my nephew?"

There was no mistaking now the little note of triumph in Tamara's voice as she replied:

"My father, Your Grace, was an Oxford Don. He was a Classical scholar with a great reputation. He published eight books on the Classics which are very highly spoken of by experts!"

As Tamara spoke she thought that she had meant to confound him and succeeded.

At the same time she could not help a little tremor of fear in case she had gone too far and he would dismiss her instantly because she had defied him.

Instead after a moment he said:

"You have certainly given me a great deal of information that I had not expected, Miss Wynne. Now shall we return to the present problem? I am sure you have many suggestions as to how the children's position in the household could be improved."

"I would like to suggest first, Your Grace, that we are moved to a different part of the Castle," Tamara said quickly. "The children have been used to living with their parents and they always occupied the best rooms in their house in Cornwall.

"They will do no damage, that I promise you, but there must be rooms which are more congenial than the dilapidated Nurseries where we are housed at the moment."

"I take your point, Miss Wynne," the Duke said coldly.

"And I think it would be a good idea if we were allowed a small Dining-Room nearer to the kitchens so that the food will not be cold when we receive it," Tamara said. "And if I might be allowed to suggest menus which are suitable for children and good for their health, it would save a great deal of future argument."

"Anything else?" the Duke enquired.

Tamara drew in her breath.

"You know how much the children want to ride, and as an outstanding horseman yourself you will understand how frustrating it is to see other people well-mounted while being only in the position of an onlooker."

"I have a feeling, Miss Wynne, that you are pleading not

only on behalf of the children, but also on behalf of yourself."

"I am ... teaching Vava to ride," Tamara answered.

"There are plenty of horses in the stables," the Duke said, "and I imagine that you and Sándor could exercise them quite as well as any of my grooms. I will see if something can be done about acquiring ponies for the two little girls."

Tamara's eyes lit up.

"Do you mean that? Do you really mean it? It would mean more to them than anything else and help them to forget that they have lost their father and mother."

There was a soft note in her voice that had not been there before and the Duke said:

"I hope, Miss Wynne, that when all these innovations are put into practice you will be satisfied."

Once again she knew he was mocking her and she answered:

"There is one more thing, Your Grace."

"What is it now?"

"You will not forget that Sándor should go to school? He needs companions of his own age as well as lessons."

"I have already said that I will give it my consideration."

"Then I can only thank you for being so generous."

Tamara curtsied, conscious as she did so that the Duke's eyes were on her face. Then as she turned to walk away he said:

"Your father's books were of course written under his name? I shall make enquiries to see if I have any of them in my Library. If not, it is an omission which should be remedied."

For a moment Tamara held her breath, then because she could think of nothing to say she curtsied again.

"I thank Your Grace," she murmured.

As she walked away she thought wildly that she had made an irrevocable slip and unerringly the Duke had put his

80

finger on it.

As she ran upstairs to the children she was thrilled at what she had to tell them, but at the same time she could not help thinking how foolish of her it had been to say it was her father who was the Don at Oxford.

Why had she not said her uncle, or some other relative?

However the Duke knew so little about her sister that it was extremely doubtful if he knew that her name had been Selincourt.

'I won the battle on so many points,' she thought, 'but I have left myself very vulnerable, and he may shoot me down at any moment!'

It was a disquieting thought but for the moment she set it aside because she was so excited at being able to tell the children about the horses.

With a slightly better grace, although it was obvious she was somewhat affronted by the instructions she had received, Mrs. Henderson moved Tamara and the children downstairs into the West Wing.

The rooms were large and attractively furnished.

There was a delightful Sitting-Room overlooking the front of the Castle, the lake and the Park and a separate bed-room for each one of them.

"This is better!" Sándor exclaimed. "I can watch the deer from here."

"I can watch them too," Vava cried, "but I would rather see the horses."

"So would I," Sándor said with a grin.

When Tamara told him that the Duke had promised they could ride his horses, he had flung his arms around her.

"It was wonderful of you, Aunt Tamara, to make him agree," he cried.

Because she too was so excited, she forgot to rebuke him for not calling her Miss Wynne.

"The Adam Dining-Room is to be at your disposal, Miss," Mrs. Henderson said in a repressed voice, "and I understand that one of my housemaids is to be allotted to these rooms. There will also be a footman to wait upon you at meal-times."

"The Duke is doing us royally," Tamara said to Sándor when Mrs. Henderson left them.

"So he ought," Sándor answered. "After all, if he died I should be the Duke!"

Tamara looked at him in a startled fashion.

"I never thought of that!"

"Of course I would," Sándor answered. "Papa was his heir until he died. He once showed me the family-tree we had at home, and now that Papa is dead I would be the next Duke."

"I should not think about it too much," Tamara advised. "After all, the Duke is still young. He may marry and have ten of his own children!"

Sándor grinned.

"There is plenty of room for them in the Castle!"

Tamara laughed.

"To-morrow I am going to climb to the top of the tower," Sándor told her.

"You must be very careful," Tamara answered.

"I will," Sándor promised. "I do not want to have a broken leg and not be able to ride."

The children could talk of nothing else but their riding and Vava asked over and over again how soon she would have her pony.

"We will go to the stables and talk to Abbey about it to-morrow morning," Tamara promised.

But it was hard to get either Kadine or Vava to sleep because they were so thrilled at what lay ahead.

The two little girls had milk and biscuits for supper after their big tea, but Sándor and Tamara went downstairs to the

Adam Dining-Room.

Because she always changed for dinner Tamara put on one of her pretty gowns and arranged her hair in her usual style, certain that she was unlikely to meet the Duke again during the evening.

The dinner was very different from the meals they had previously endured. Tamara had the idea that it was identical to what the Duke was enjoying in the Dining-Room.

When they had finished Sándor said:

"It is warm to-night. Do you think we could go outside and walk in the garden before we go upstairs?"

Tamara smiled at him.

"It is a good idea. It is not yet dark, so we will not fall over the flower-beds or end up in the lake."

They let themselves out of a side door and walked across the lawns that were like velvet beneath their feet.

There was the scent of stock and lavender on the air and the pigeons were going to roost in the high trees in the wood.

There was a golden glow in the sky where the sun was setting on the horizon.

The Castle seemed very high and mysterious with just one or two lights showing in the downstairs windows.

Sándor ran ahead and Tamara paused in the rose garden beside a sunken pool filled with gold-fish. She watched their glimmering golden bodies as they moved amongst the flat green water-lily leaves.

It was all so beautiful she felt as if her heart went out to so much loveliness and she became a part of it.

Then suddenly a voice beside her said:

"You look like a goddess of the night, only far more desirable!"

She turned and saw the gentleman who had been with the Duke in the stable-yard.

He came far too close to her and she moved a step away from him.

83

"Sándor and I were just returning to the Castle," she said quickly.

As she spoke she looked for Sándor, but there was no sign of him.

"There is no hurry," the gentleman said.

"I have things to see to indoors, Sir."

"Not so fast," he answered, "we have not yet been formerly introduced. My name is Cropthorne, Lord Cropthorne – and yours?"

"Miss Wynne . . . and I am the children's Governess as Your Lordship is well aware."

He laughed.

"You are trying to put me in my place. But your lips are far too attractive to speak in such a severe tone. They were meant for kisses, not for rebukes."

"I would thank Your Lordship not to speak to me in such a manner," Tamara answered coldly.

She would have walked away, but he reached out and took hold of her wrist.

"I shall talk to you as I like," he said. "How could I have expected to find anything so lovely and so very alluring in Granchester's gloomy Castle?"

"Let me go!" Tamara said sharply.

"On one condition," he answered.

She did not reply and he said:

"I will tell you what it is – that you let me kiss you as I have desired to do ever since I saw you this afternoon."

"I have no intention of allowing you to do any such thing," Tamara said angrily. "You will please let loose my wrist at once. I cannot believe that the Duke would think it commendable of you to behave in such a manner."

"Has the Duke a prior claim?" Lord Cropthorne asked.

In answer Tamara struggled to free herself, but he held on to her and laughed softly.

"I have no intention of letting you go, you glorious creature," he said. "I have a penchant for women with large, dark eyes and red hair. They are more quickly aroused than their paler sisters."

As he spoke he drew Tamara relentlessly towards him.

She knew that in a battle of strength she would be helpless.

At the same time she found herself suddenly panic-stricken at the thought of what he intended to do.

He was the type of raffish Rake that she had written about in her novel, but had never actually encountered in real life.

Now she knew this was just the sort of situation in which her villainous Duke had been involved, and which had disgusted her even as she wrote about it.

She struggled but Lord Cropthorne's arms were round her, and although she twisted her head away from him she felt it was only a question of time before he overpowered her.

Then she had an idea!

For one moment she let herself go limp in his arms, so limp that he thought he had triumphed and his lips were on her cheek.

Then with all her strength she pushed him away from her. His feet slipped on the paving-stones around the water-lily pool and he fell backwards into it with a loud splash.

Tamara did not wait even to see what had happened but turned and ran, hearing a string of oaths as she went.

Reaching the lawn she sped across it towards the Castle only to run full tilt into someone whom she had not seen in the shadow of the building.

Only as she was halted violently by the contact and put out her hands to save herself did she realise it was the Duke.

His hands steadied her. Then as she gasped for breath he said in his most sarcastic tone:

"You appear to be in somewhat of a hurry, Miss Wynne. What can have caused such impetuosity?"

Tamara forgot everything but her anger at what had happened.

She pulled herself out of the Duke's arms and said in a voice which strove to be disdainful, but which in reality was very young and breathless:

"You will find your . . . friend . . . Your Grace, in the water-lily pool . . . and I hope he . . . drowns!"

With that she walked into the Castle without looking back.

Only as she reached the Sitting-Room in the West Wing did she wonder what the Duke had thought and told herself furiously that it was of no consequence.

He could hardly dismiss her for resenting the advances of his guest, even if her behaviour was unconventional.

At the same time she was afraid he might be persuaded that it was her fault for having encouraged Lord Cropthorne in some way or other.

She was standing at the window trying to collect her scattered thoughts and breathe more naturally when Sándor came into the room.

"Where did you get to?" he asked. "I went back to find you at the water-lily pool, but the gentleman who is staying with the Duke was standing in the middle of it, and he was swearing, as Papa would have said, like a trooper! I have never heard such a string of oaths!"

"Was the Duke with him?" Tamara asked.

"He was standing beside the pool," Sándor said, "and what do you think? He was laughing! I never thought he could laugh – he seemed stiff and starchy."

"He was . . . laughing!" Tamara repeated.

It was of course absurd of her but she was relieved that the Duke was not angry but amused.

The following morning Tamara went to the stables wearing her riding-habit and she and Sándor were mounted by Abbey on two of the fine horses which filled the Duke's stables.

A young groom rode beside Kadine with her horse on a

leading rein and old Abbey himself took charge of Vava.

"Don't worrit about th' young ladies, Miss," he said to Tamara. "You have a good gallop with Master Sándor, and Oi'll look after 'em 'till ye returns."

"You are to do exactly what Abbey tells you," Tamara admonished the two little girls. She was as excited as Sándor as they set off across the Park.

They rode for about two miles, then turned their horses for home.

"I am beginning to feel glad that we came to the Castle," Sándor said. "I thought at first that I was going to hate it."

"So did I," Tamara replied, "but being able to ride horses like these makes up for a lot of other things."

"Even for the odious advances of Lord Cropthorne," she told herself.

She had felt a little guilty when she went to bed and thought over what had occurred.

Then she decided he had thoroughly deserved what she had done to him.

He was, she was sure, the type of roué who thought that unprotected governesses and young housemaids were fair game. But Tamara hoped she had taught him a lesson.

However much she disliked the Duke, she could not believe he would behave in such a despicable manner.

'He would be too proud to condescend to a creature so much below him in social standing as a Governess!' she thought.

That might be reassuring; at the same time it was depressing to think that in the whole Castle there was no-one she could turn to as an equal and a friend.

In fact she had an idea that she was going to find it very lonely with no-one to talk to.

They did not see the Duke that day.

In the afternoon Tamara collected some books from the Library and took them up to their Sitting-Room.

There had been a wide variety of choice which had delighted her. At the same time she knew she was going to miss discussing what she read with Lord Ronald as she had done in Cornwall.

Maïka was as well educated as herself and they had often read together books in French, in Italian and Hungarian.

"It would be a shame for us to forget Mama's native tongue," Maïka had said often enough, "or to become too English."

She smiled as she spoke and added:

"Ronald said he fell in love with me because I looked different from any other girl he had ever seen, and he likes me when I am wildly Hungarian and unpredictable."

"I, on the other hand," Tamara told herself, "have now to be very English."

She could not forget the disparaging note in the Duke's voice when he had spoken of her being foreign.

'He is ridiculously insular,' she thought.

Somehow she could not help thinking about him even though she hated him.

But she was beginning to realise that she was not the only person in the Castle or outside who disliked the Duke.

It was obvious that the servants were not fond of him, as the servants in Cornwall had loved her sister and brother-in-law. She had learnt too from old Abbey that there was trouble on the Estate.

It was just something he had said rather vaguely, but she asked:

"Are you having riots and protests in this part of the country as I believe there has been in other places?"

"We 'as our difficulties," Abbey said in a rather repressed manner which made her think he could say more if he wished to do so.

"You mean there is unrest amongst the labourers?"

"They 'as their grievances an' there's not enough police-men t' stop 'em here as there be in London."

"Have they taken their complaints to His Grace?" Tamara asked.

"Aye, an' he'll not listen to them! But Oi thinks afore Oi gets much older that th' landlords 'll have t' listen, as those as be in Parliament 'll have t' listen sooner or later!"

Tamara was surprised that in Gloucester of all places there should be unrest.

She knew from what she had read in the newspapers and from what Lord Ronald had told her that the working conditions both in towns and in the country the previous year had caused riots which seemed to verge on revolution.

In August a meeting of malcontents had taken place at St. Peter's Fields in Manchester resulting in what had been called "The Battle of Peterloo".

Hundreds of unarmed men, women and children had been cut down by the sabres of mounted yeomanry and left wounded or dead.

The event had shocked the whole country and evoked a class-hatred which Lord Ronald was certain would recoil on the Landed Proprietors and the Mill owners for years, if not for generations.

It had all begun with the growing concern about the terrible crimes against children that were taking place in the great cities like London.

Tamara had heard of the 'Flash Houses', of the iniquitous treatment of sweeping-boys, the growing numbers of child prostitutes which were a disgrace to any civilised or Christian country.

But she had not thought this would particularly concern people who lived in out-lying districts until she learnt that injustice and low wages had caused revolts and riots amongst the country labourers also.

Ricks had been set on fire and the leaders when they were caught had been savagely punished and either hanged or transported.

She wondered what the Duke's attitude was to all these things.

She could not help thinking that by his very arrogance and the manner in which he seemed to look with disdain on those who were weaker than himself, he would incur their enmity.

She found that after the Duke had read the newspapers the day they arrived, she could obtain them next day from the Curator in the Library.

She read the Parliamentary debates and the reports of what was happening in other parts of the country and wondered if the Duke, being such a large land-owner, was perturbed about what might happen on his own Estate.

She talked to the old Curator, but he was concerned only with the Castle and its contents and she had the idea that he had long since ceased to realise that a world existed outside it.

She did not see Lord Cropthorne again and learnt that he had left the Castle.

While she half-expected the Duke to rebuke her for her behaviour towards his friend, she learnt from the servants that he had gone away that day with friends.

It made her feel that she and the children now had a freedom to move about in a way they had not been able to do before. They explored the great State Rooms, the Chapel, the Orangery, the Ball Room, and of course the Norman tower which for Sándor had a fascination all of its own.

"If we had other children we could play 'hide-and-seek'," Kadine said rather wistfully.

"It is certainly an idea," Tamara replied. "We shall have to find out if there are any local children we can ask to tea."

She thought that Kadine and Vava were rather bored with the tour of the Castle, so the next day she suggested that they should go down to the hay-field and take a picnic tea with them.

Their footman, who by this time was only too willing to do anything Tamara suggested, brought them a picnic basket and they set off, the little girls wearing their sun-bonnets and Tamara carrying her sunshade.

Hay-making had always been a time for festivity in Cornwall.

The children loved to help, or more often hinder, the women who turned the corn and stacked it in what they described as small wigwams so that it could dry out in the sun.

A large field which they found beyond the gardens had been cut, but the hay had been left to dry in the sun and there was no-one there but themselves.

Sándor started to tease Kadine by throwing hay at her, Tamata joined in and they all pelted each other until finally as Tamara sat down exhausted the children began to bury her in the hay, shouting with delight as they did so.

She was almost completely buried and she had shut her eyes against the stalks which tickled her face when she heard Sándor exclaim:

"Hello, Uncle Howard! We thought you had gone away."

"I have returned," the Duke replied.

Tamara sat up.

Beside them was the Duke riding one of his fine horses and she was immediately conscious of how undignified she must look up to her chin in hay!

There were pieces of it in her hair which, while she was playing, had lost its pins and was falling over her shoulders like a red tide.

She rose, shaking her skirt as she did so and trying to pull pieces of hay out of her hair.

"You appear to be enjoying yourself, Miss Wynne," the Duke remarked.

She did not reply and after a moment he said:

"Have you no complaints? I can hardly believe that my

hay, if nothing else, is to your satisfaction."

Tamara pulled back her hair and tried to twist it in a bun at the back of her neck as she replied:

"I have not only no complaints, Your Grace, but a great deal for which to thank you. We have all ridden these last two mornings and enjoyed it exceedingly."

"I find that most reassuring, Miss Wynne."

He was being sarcastic but Tamara was too conscious of her appearance to feel defiant.

"I can ride," Vava said suddenly. "I can ride, Uncle Howard, a horse as big as yours!"

Before the Duke could reply Sándor said:

"I, too, would like to thank you, Uncle Howard. It is thrilling to ride your horses, and I know Papa would be pleased that you are so kind to us."

"That is not the reputation I usually have," the Duke answered.

Without another word he rode away.

"He really is the most exasperating and unpredictable man," Tamara said to herself angrily. "He turns up when he is least expected and behaves in a manner in which no other man would."

She had a feeling that he was watching her.

Perhaps he wanted to find an excuse for dismissing her from her post or maybe he resented the criticisms she had made and was determined to fault her.

Whatever the reason he made her feel uneasy.

Somehow the excitement had gone from the afternoon, and even when they had their tea in the shade of a tree the sunshine seemed a little dimmed and their laughter not so frequent.

'The Duke spoils everything!' Tamara thought petulantly.

She told herself there was no doubt that there was a very close resemblance between him and the fictitious Duke of Ullester in her novel.

CHAPTER FIVE

Tamara rode into the stable-yard with Kadine at her side.

They had been in the Park together and Kadine was now allowed to ride without a leading rein, as she had a pony of her own.

It was a nice, quiet animal and a little bigger than the one that Abbey had found for Vava.

Kadine enjoyed riding, but she was not adventurous like Sándor or obsessed with it like Vava.

"You rode very well, darling," Tamara said.

Kadine smiled at her, looking so pretty as she did so that Tamara thought again how irresistible she would be when she grew up.

Old Abbey and Vava were outside the pony's stall. Vava as usual was refusing to dismount, insisting that she wanted to go on riding.

"Hurry up, Vava!" Tamara said as a groom helped her from her own horse. "It is time for tea."

"I do not want any tea," Vava said obstinately, "I want to go back and look at the little piebald pony."

Tamara looked at Abbey enquiringly and he explained:

"There's some gypsies at th' far end o' the Park, Miss, and Miss Vava was taken with a small piebald foal they've got there."

"It was so pretty!" Vava cried, "I want it! I want it all for my own!"

"That is greedy," Tamara replied, lifting Vava down from the saddle. "You have Butterfly, and no-one could have a nicer or prettier pony."

"I want two ponies!" Vava insisted.

"You are asking too much!" Tamara said firmly, "and I know you love Butterfly."

Vava kissed her pony's nose and gave it a piece of carrot which one of the stable-boys had ready.

Tamara was just about to take her away when she saw Major Melville coming down the yard towards them.

He was a middle-aged man who had been Comptroller to the previous Duke and had therefore lived at the Castle for many years.

Since he had returned Tamara found that everyhing seemed to be running more smoothly, the servants were more obliging, and she was quite certain that the Duke found him irreplaceable.

"Good afternoon, Miss Wynne," Major Melville said raising his hat.

"Good afternoon, Major, we have all had a most enjoyable ride, and it is a lovely day."

"I want a horse, please, Abbey," Major Melville said to the groom.

"At once, Sir," Abbey replied. "Will ye be a-going far?"

"No, only to the end of the Park. His Grace wants me to turn away the gypsies."

"Turn away the gypsies?" Tamara exclaimed. "But why?"

"You must not send them away!" Vava cried leaving Butterfly and running to Major Melville's side. "They have a dear little piebald pony and I want him all for my own."

"His Grace does not wish the gypsies to camp in the Park," Major Melville said to Tamara.

"They've come here for many a year, Sir," Old Abbey remarked, "an' they don't make no trouble. They're on th' way t' Evesham for the fruit picking."

"I am aware of that, Abbey," Major Melville replied, "but I have my orders."

As he spoke a horse which had been saddled was brought from its stall and he mounted it.

"You are not to send away the piebald pony!" Vava cried.

Major Melville merely smiled at her, then lifting his hat to Tamara he rode away.

"Why does the Duke not like gypsies?" Kadine asked as Tamara and the two little girls walked back to the Castle.

"I do not know," Tamara answered. "We used to see them in Cornwall, if you remember."

"Mumma always bought clothes-pegs from them," Kadine said, "and they had pretty painted caravans. I thought I would like to live in one."

"You would find it very cramped after your big bed-room here," Tamara smiled.

"It would be fun in the summer," Kadine said, "but perhaps rather cold in the winter, except that gypsies always have big fires."

Vava was silent. Tamara thought it was because she was thinking of the little piebald pony and changed the subject.

She knew, if Vava became interested in some particular object, how she would talk about it incessantly, which at times could be very wearying.

Tea was waiting for them upstairs in their Sitting-Room and Tamara noticed with satisfaction that it was a very different meal from what they had been given when they first arrived.

The Chef had gradually mellowed towards the children, and now there was not only a variety of cakes and scones for tea and little coloured jellies but also fruit from the garden and thick cream.

Tamara looked at the clock and realised they had been riding rather later than usual and that Sándor should be home soon.

When Major Melville had returned to the Castle the Duke had obviously spoken to him about Sándor's education. She was informed he would attend a local school and he had started at the beginning of the week.

He had not said very much when he returned the first two evenings, but yesterday Tamara had thought that he seemed unusually silent and had lost his high spirits.

She supposed it was because he was finding it strange to be amongst other boys and thought he would naturally take a little time to settle down.

She had hoped that the Duke would suggest sending him to a Boarding School like Eton or Harrow.

But she thought perhaps the day-school was only a preliminary experiment and it would be a mistake for her to say too much until she saw how Sándor got on.

Kadine and Vava finished their tea but there was still no sign of their brother.

They played for a while with their toys. Then as Vava seemed to be tired Tamara called Rose, the maid who looked after them and suggested the little girl should be put to bed.

"Shall I read you a story, Kadine?" Tamara asked.

Kadine eagerly fetched a book which they had begun several days ago and which was an adventure story which she particularly enjoyed.

They were sitting on the sofa and Tamara had only read half a page when the door opened.

She looked up with a smile, knowing it must be Sándor, then gave an exclamation of horror.

He came into the room obviously walking with difficulty, and dragging one leg behind the other. His coat was torn, his shirt was open at the neck, one eye was swollen and almost closed.

There was bood running from a cut lip and his nose had been bleeding too.

"Sándor! What has happened?" Tamara exclaimed hurrying towards him.

She put her arms out as she spoke and the boy almost collapsed into them.

She helped him to the sofa and laid him down, fetching a cup of milk from the tea-table, and holding it to his lips.

He found it hard to drink and after a few sips he waved it away and shut his eyes.

She took off his shoes, noting they were dusty and scratched, then fetched some warm water to bathe his eye and his lip.

It was some time later when he seemed a little relaxed that she said to him quietly:

"Tell me, darling, what happened?"

. . .

Tamara ran down the front stairs and across the Hall.

She did not wait to ask a footman where the Duke was likely to be, because she was quite certain that at this time in the evening he would be in the Blue Salon.

It was where he habitually sat reading the newspapers which did not arrive at the Castle until the afternoon.

Her eyes were stormy and her lips were in a tight line, and anyone who knew her would have been aware that Tamara's Hungarian temper was flaring as fiery as the hair on her head.

She walked into the Blue Salon but the Duke was not there.

Then as she paused, wondering where she should look for him, she heard the sound of voices and realised a door which communicated with the Study next door was ajar.

She walked towards it and was just about to pull the door further open when she heard Major Melville say:

"If you sued the author of this iniquitous book I am quite certain, Your Grace, you would get very substantial damages – certainly not less than £5,000, I should imagine."

"You are right, Melville," the Duke replied. "I have never in my life read anything so scurrilous or so poisonously offensive!"

97

The Duke paused, then added:

"I wonder who the author is? The mere initials 'T.S.' might hide the identity of a man or a woman."

"I hardly think, Your Grace, that a woman would be so vitriolic."

"One never knows," the Duke answered. "There are some women who, when it suits them, can be just as spiteful as any man."

"I will take Your Grace's word for it," Major Melville replied, "but what steps shall I take on your behalf?"

There was silence and Tamara held her breath.

She was only too well aware what they were discussing.

Yesterday she had received a letter forwarded to her by Mr. Lawson from her Publishers.

They informed her that her instructions to withdraw the book had arrived after the novel had actually been distributed to the book-sellers and there was therefore nothing they could do about it.

They had gone on to say:

"We deeply regret, Madam, that you wish to take this step seeing that in our opinion the novel will sell well and in fact we are quite certain that in a month's time we shall be obliged to re-print it.

In the meantime we enclose a cheque for £20 for advance sales which we hope will be to your satisfaction."

Tamara had read the letter and was upset and somewhat perturbed by the information it contained.

"There is nothing I can do about it," she told herself. "At the same time I hope the book will not sell and no-one will give the Duke a copy."

It had been one thing to write about him in a vitriolic manner when she had never seen him, and she had thought when she first came to the Castle that every word her book contained was fully justified.

But as time passed she had found it increasingly hard to go on disliking him so violently, when he had allowed her to ride, given the children ponies, and acquiesced in her demands regarding their accommodation and food.

She still thought he was overwhelmingly autocratic, that he looked on her in a disdainful manner and was waiting to find fault.

But she had to admit if she was honest that he had, once they had settled in, not been half as much of an ogre as she had expected him to be.

She had looked again at the Solicitor's letter and walked to the window to look out at the beauty of the lake outside and wonder if truthfully she could say she was sorry she had come to the Castle.

"He will never read the book," she told herself reassuringly.

It was a statement that seemed to repeat and re-repeat itself in her brain.

Now she was proved to be wrong.

The Duke had read her novel and it was quite obvious what he thought about it.

"I have been sent copies of this scurrilous novel by three people already," she heard him say slowly. "Two of them are relations who are furious that what they call 'the family honour' should be dragged in the mud and the other is a friend who has offered to horse-whip both the author and the Publisher."

"I think you should take some action, Your Grace."

"On the other hand, as you well know, Melville, to bring a case like this into Court is to give the author, who is obviously an extremely unpleasant individual, just the sort of publicity he would wish to have."

"You can hardly let the whole thing pass without making a protest," Major Melville answered.

"No, I realise that," the Duke replied, "and I have decided

what I shall do."

"What is that, Your Grace?"

"You will send to London immediately and buy up every available copy of the book. Take over the Publisher's stock, search the book-sellers for every unsold volume and have them brought back here."

"What will you do with them all, Your Grace?"

"Burn them!" the Duke answered. "It is the only way to dispose of filth!"

"It will cost a considerable sum of money."

"That is completely immaterial," the Duke replied, "but make it quite clear to the Publishers that if they bring out another edition I will sue them for every penny they possess."

There was a forceful determination in the Duke's voice which Tamara had heard before.

Then so suddenly that she started nervously he walked in to the Blue Salon through the half-open door to find her just on the other side of it.

"You wanted to see me, Miss Wynne?"

"Yes, Your Grace."

He shut the door behind him and made a gesture towards one of the sofas.

"Will you sit down?"

"No!"

He raised his eye-brows and stood facing her, an enigmatic expression on his face.

"What is it?" he asked.

"Sándor – he has just returned from school. I wish Your Grace to see the state he is in."

The Duke smiled cynically.

"He has been fighting, I suppose. Do not distress yourself. All boys fight and I expect it will take him a little time to find his own level."

Tamara drew in her breath.

"He has come back in a state of collapse. I think several of

100

his ribs may be broken and he cannot see out of one eye."

"Sándor is growing up and he has to fight his own battles," the Duke said indifferently.

"I agree he has to fight his *own* battles," Tamara said sharply, "but not yours."

"What do you mean by that?"

"Sándor has been deliberately beaten up because of you and your behaviour."

She spoke rudely but she did not care.

The Duke's indifference was the last straw and her feeling of fury at what had happened to Sándor grew.

He had not wanted to tell her about it but she had coaxed it out of him because she had to know.

She could not bear to have him treated in such a way and not understand the cause of it.

"Are you telling me that Sándor has been fighting to save my good name?" the Duke asked mockingly.

It was the last straw which broke through Tamara's effort at self-control.

Her eyes flashed and her words when she replied came tumbling through her lips as if she could no longer suppress them.

"Sándor was deliberately set upon by three boys older and bigger than himself who had been told by their fathers to take it out on him because they hate you!"

"Hate me?" the Duke asked.

"Does that surprise you?" Tamara asked. "You must realise that there are a great number of people who hate you, but there is no reason why Sándor should be practically murdered in consequence."

"I can hardly credit what you are telling me," the Duke said.

"Then perhaps you will remember turning a tenant-farmer off your land because you said he did not farm well enough? His son was one of the boys who attacked Sándor."

101

She saw the Duke knew who the man was she had mentioned.

"Another was the son of the local saddler," she went on, "whose bill you refused to pay for what you called inferior workmanship. The third, was the son of your butcher, whom you accused of overcharging."

Tamara paused for breath, then she continued:

"Sándor's wounds will heal, but I am wondering why, unless you were striking at your brother through his son, you sent him to such a school."

She saw the anger in the Duke's face, but she stormed on:

"I asked you to send Sándor to school so that he could have proper companionship. Do you really consider such boys the right companions for your nephew and heir? If so, are you prepared to entertain them here at the Castle and invite their fathers to come with them?"

Tamara's voice seemed to ring out.

When she finished speaking there was silence, a silence when she and the Duke stood looking at each other, both with their eyes dark with anger.

Tamara's hands were clenched and her whole body tense. Then as she waited for his reply to her challenge he turned away and walked across the room.

"I will see Sándor for myself," he said and crossing the Hall walked slowly up the staircase.

Tamara was trembling and was so shaken with fury that for the moment she could not follow him.

"I am glad I wrote my novel!" she told herself. "I am glad it shocked and affronted him! Perhaps now he will realise that he is just as horrible as the Duke of Ullester – in fact he is worse!"

It was a few minutes before she could force herself to leave the Blue Salon and walk up the stairs. Then as she moved slowly towards the West Wing she encountered Mrs. Henderson.

"Oh, Miss Wynne! I've never heard such a thing, I haven't really!" the Housekeeper cried. "Poor young gentleman, it's a crying shame, that's what it is! But there, I always knew that school was full of a lot of rough, common boys. I can't understand His Grace sending Master Sándor there, that I can't!"

"I shall not let him go there again, Mrs. Henderson," Tamara assured her.

She was not surprised at the Housekeeper's agitation over Sándor because now she had got used to the children there was no doubt that he was her favourite and could do no wrong in her eyes.

"I'm just going downstairs, Miss Wynne," Mrs. Henderson continued, "to tell the Chef to make some nourishing soup for the poor little fellow. He'll not be able to eat anything solid."

"No, I am afraid not," Tamara agreed. "I had intended to ask the Chef myself for a bowl of soup but it would be very kind if you could do it for me."

"It's a pleasure, Miss Wynne," the Housekeeper said. "And I've some salve in my room which I'm sure would help Master Sándor's bruises. I've used it many a time and very efficacious it's proved."

"Thank you very much, Mrs. Henderson."

The Housekeeper hurried away, her chatelaine clanking, her black dress rustling.

She had certainly changed from the woman who had refused to have the Nurseries cleaned and had thought the better rooms were too good for the children.

Tamara reached the part they occupied in the West Wing, but she did not go into the Sitting-Room.

She could hear the Duke's deep voice speaking to Sándor, and she went first to say good-night to Vava only to find her asleep, then into Kadine's room.

"You have been a long time coming to me," Kadine said.

"As you could not go on reading the book, will you tell me a story?"

"A very short one," Tamara replied.

It was a story that Kadine particularly liked about a little girl who had the most fantastic adventures. She encountered giants and dragons, was assisted by a number of good fairies, and escaped in dark woods from goblins and witches.

It was difficult for Tamara to tell the story with her mind on Sándor and while she was seething with anger against the Duke.

But she forced herself to concentrate and as the story wound to a dramatic climax she realised that Kadine's eyes were dropping, and as she finished the last word the child was asleep.

It was only then she realised they were not alone in the bed-room for standing by the open doorway was the Duke.

She looked at him and knew that he intended to speak to her.

She put her fingers up to her lips, tucked the sheet under Kadine's chin, then rose to lower the blind over the open window.

Very softly she went out of the room and the Duke followed her.

"I want to speak to you, Miss Wynne."

She stood waiting and he said:

"Shall we go into the Sitting-Room? I have carried Sándor to his own bed."

"You carried him?"

"He was not too heavy for me," the Duke replied sarcastically.

Tamara did not answer. She was surprised that the Duke should concern himself so closely with one of the children, especially Sándor.

She walked into the Sitting-Room and as the Duke followed her he said:

"I sent for Watkins, my own valet, who actually is an extremely good nurse and told him to undress Sándor. He will, I assure you, do it as gently as any woman could."

"I suppose I should thank Your Grace."

"That is quite unnecessary," the Duke answered, "but I am, although you may not believe it, extremely perturbed at the state the boy is in."

"I am very glad to hear it."

As she spoke she suddenly realised she should not speak to the Duke in such a way.

After all, she was supposed to be a humble and subservient Governess, a servant he could dismiss at a moment's notice without a reference if she offended him.

Because she knew she could not bear to leave the children she forced herself to say in a somewhat milder tone:

"I hope Your Grace will now realise that your choice of a school was at fault?"

"I am aware of that, Miss Wynne, and I have told Sándor so," the Duke answered. "He will go to Eton at the beginning of next term, and I wish to consult you as to which tutors you consider are necessary to teach him until September."

"You will send him to Eton?" Tamara asked.

"I have promised him that I will do so."

"It is where Lord Ronald went and where I always wanted him to go."

"As it happens, it is also where I was educated," the Duke answered.

"Then why . . . ?" Tamara began.

She saw the expression on his face and the words died away from her lips.

"All right," the Duke said in an irritated tone. "I made a mistake, and I am not too proud to admit it. If you want to know the truth, I resented the fact that you assumed that I should automatically take over the upbringing of these children."

105

"It was because there . . . seemed to be . . . no-one else," Tamara answered weakly.

She suddenly saw that she had been very demanding and peremptory. Because Mr. Lawson had convinced her there was nowhere else they could go she had been concerned only in forcing the Duke, whom she hated, into doing what she wanted.

"There are actually quite a number of relations who would have been only too pleased to more or less adopt my brother's children," the Duke said, "but you did not think to discuss it with me, Miss Wynne."

"What you are implying, Your Grace, is that what has happened to Sándor is my fault."

"In a way," the Duke answered, then he smiled.

She looked at him in surprise because the anger had gone from his face and instead his eyes were twinkling.

"May I say, Miss Wynne, that you are not only a very formidable opponent, but also a fanatical champion of those you love."

Tamara could think of no reply and as she looked at him uncertainly he went from the Sitting-Room leaving her alone.

She ran to Sándor's room.

The Duke's valet, Watkins, was with him, a small elderly man who had always been very polite although until now they had had little to do with him.

"I've got him into bed, Miss," he said to Tamara in a conspiratorial whisper. "The poor young gentleman's going to be black and blue to-morrow, but if you ask me there's no bones broken."

"Are you sure of that?" Tamara asked. "He has a pain in his ribs and I thought one might be fractured."

"He were punched pretty hard, Miss, but I'm thinking it's his eye that'll hurt him most. I'm just a-going downstairs to get a compress. If there isn't any ice in the Castle I'll send to the ice-house down by the lake."

"It is very kind of you," Tamara said.

"It reminds me of when His Grace and Master Ronald were young. They beat up some village lads as was shooting at the deer with bows and arrows. There were two of them against half-a-dozen."

"Who won?" Tamara asked.

"They did, Miss, but His Grace had an eye as black as coal and Master Ronald had his arm in a sling for over a week!"

The old man chuckled.

"But there, Miss, boys will be boys!"

He hurried away to get the compress and Tamara went to Sándor's side.

"Are you all right, dearest?" she asked feeling the tears rise in her eyes as she looked down at his battered face.

"Uncle Howard was jolly kind," he answered. "He says I need not go back to that beastly school and he is sending me to Eton."

"I know," Tamara said, "and that is where I always wanted you to go."

"And Papa would have liked that!"

"He would, and your mother as well."

Sándor tried to smile and failed.

"Not Mama," he said. "She never wanted any of us to go away from home, but I expect I would have gone all the same."

"I am sure you would," Tamara agreed, "and Sándor, although it has been a horrible experience, you must forget about it. We all make mistakes and going to that school was one of them."

"That is what Uncle Howard said. Do you know, he sort of apologised for sending me there! That was jolly big of him, wasn't it?"

"Yes . . . I suppose it was," Tamara said slowly.

There was a silence while Sándor closed his eyes, but a minute or so later he said:

"I thought when we first came here that I hated him, but now in lots of ways I think he is rather like Papa."

When Sándor had finally been settled for the night, Tamara left a bell by his bed so that he could ring for her if he wanted anything.

She walked into the Sitting-Room and for the first time she could think of her book and what she had overheard the Duke saying to Major Melville.

She felt guilty about the cheque for £20 which she had hidden in her bed-room and thought perhaps she should return it.

But she remembered that the Duke had told Major Melville to buy up all the books which were in the shops and the Publisher's stock. That meant that neither the Publishers nor the book-sellers would suffer any financial loss.

"I will spend most of the money on the children and the rest on charity," Tamara told herself.

It would be a salve for her conscience if she did not keep anything for herself.

She thought of the terms in which the Duke had described the book and its author and felt ashamed.

It was only because she had been so incensed at the way her sister and her brother-in-law had been treated that she had tried to avenge them in the only way open to her.

When she was writing 'The Ducal Wasp', she had no idea she would ever meet the real Duke of Granchester or even see him for that matter.

It had just been a blow struck at a shadowy figure, and yet now the whole thing had come back on her in a way that was frightening.

She gave a deep sigh and told herself that whatever happened the Duke must never find out.

There was no reason why 'T.S.' should mean anything to him, yet Tamara wished she had used an entirely fictitious name. She had signed her first book with initials hoping that the critics would think she was a man.

But here was another pit-fall, she told herself, which might, if she was not careful, reveal her identity not only as the author of the 'most poisonous and scurrilous' novel the Duke had ever read, but also a governess.

She felt herself tremble at the thought of what would happen should she be unmasked.

It would certainly, she thought, give the Duke the excuse he needed to throw her ignominiously out of the Castle and out of the children's lives.

She felt suddenly horrified at how rude she had been to him when she told him of Sándor's disastrous ordeal.

But it was impossible to control her anger when she thought of how reprehensible it had been of the Duke to send Sándor to such a school.

He must have had some idea of how disliked he was in the neighbourhood.

"He cannot be so blind as to think everyone likes him," she said to herself.

Yet after all she supposed that, since he was a Duke and in a position of great authority in the County, there were few people with the exception of herself, who were likely to tell him the truth.

'That is as revolutionary as if I actually started a riot in the Castle,' she thought.

At the same time, even her triumph at obtaining the Duke's promise to send Sándor to Eton was offset by the fact that he was disgusted by her novel.

Other people would doubtless find it amusing, even while those who were spiteful would delight in the unpleasant picture it painted of the Duke of Granchester.

Suddenly Tamara remembered that the Duke had said

that two copies had been sent to him by his relatives who had been shocked at 'the family pride being dragged into the mud'.

She had forgotten, that the children were part of the family.

In disparaging the Duke and attacking him in such an obvious manner as to be recognisable, she was attacking the whole Grant family, and Sándor, Kadine and Vava were all Grants.

'I have made a mess of it,' Tamara thought humbly.

When she went to bed she lay for a long time in the darkness wishing, as so many people have wished before her, that she could put back the clock and write a very different book from the one which had been published.

Because she had been so late in going to sleep Tamara, instead of being awake when Rose the housemaid came in to pull her curtains, was still dreaming.

As the sunshine came in through the windows she sat up in bed to ask:

"What time is it, Rose?"

"Eight o'clock, Miss, and Mr. Watkins said I was to tell you that Master Sándor has had a good night and is quite comfortable this morning."

"I should be attending to him."

"Don't worry, Miss," Rose answered. "Mr. Watkins loves having someone t' nurse. He often says his talents are wasted 'cause His Grace never has a day's illness."

"No, I am sure he is very strong," Tamara answered as she got out of bed.

"Mr. Watkins nursed th' late Duke afore he died," Rose went on, "and th' old gentleman couldn't bear him out o' his sight."

"I must hurry and get dressed," Tamara said. "Would you be very kind and wake Miss Kadine and Miss Vava?"

"I'll do that, Miss."

110

It was usually Tamara who woke the little girls and had them ready to go down to breakfast at eight-thirty in the Adam Dining-Room.

But now she was just arranging her hair when Kadine knocked on the door and without waiting for an answer came running in.

"Sándor is awake, Miss Wynne, and says he wants an egg for breakfast. May he have one?"

"Yes, tell him he can have anything if he feels he can eat it," Tamara answered. "I will not be a minute."

She put a last pin into her hair and took down a light muslin gown from the wardrobe.

"Please, Kadine dearest, ask Rose to come and do me up," she said.

"Would you like me to do it?" Kadine enquired.

"I think Rose would be quicker," Tamara answered. "I am in a hurry because I overslept."

"I expect you were tired because you were worried about Sándor," Kadine said perceptively.

"That is true," Tamara smiled. "Now be a good girl and fetch Rose."

Kadine hurried away and Tamara put on her muslin gown, found her light slippers and was ready except for the fastening at the back of her dress when Rose came into the room.

"Will you do me up please, Rose?" she asked. "Is Miss Vava ready?"

"Miss Vava wasn't in her room when I goes in t' her," Rose answered.

"Then she must be with Miss Kadine."

"No, Miss Kadine hasn't seen her," Rose replied deftly fastening the buttons at the back of Tamara's gown.

"It is very naughty of her to run around before she is dressed," Tamara said. "I have told her about it before."

"Oh, she's dressed, Miss. I left a clean frock on a chair ready for her last night, an' it's gone, an' so have her shoes."

111

"I shall be very angry with her if she has gone to the stables," Tamara said. "She knows I like her to have breakfast first."

"You can't stop Miss Vava loving that pony o' hers," Rose said. "Fair dotes on it, she does!"

"I think we all want something to love," Tamara said reflectively.

"That's what my mother always used t' say, Miss. We all needs a touch of love in our lives an' without it there's only tears."

"I am sure your mother was very wise," Tamara remarked.

Then as Rose had finished doing her up she hurried from the room to see Sándor.

He was certainly better, although his eye was black and blue and his cut lip was very swollen.

"How do you feel, dearest?" Tamara asked.

"Rather sore," Sándor answered.

"If you stay quietly in your room to-day perhaps you will be able to get up to-morrow."

"If I do not have to go to school, I would much rather be riding."

"I know that," Tamara answered, "but I am afraid you would find it very uncomfortable."

"I suppose you are right," Sándor said with a sigh. "I have lots of books to read, and will you play chess with me when you have time?"

"Yes, I would rather you played games, since it is difficult to read when you have only one eye," Tamara answered. "I will play chess as soon as I have taken the girls for a walk. They can go without their lessons this morning."

"Good!" Sándor said.

Tamara put out her hand to Kadine who was hovering by the bed.

"Come along," she said, "we will go downstairs and start

our breakfast. If Vava's is cold she will have no-one to blame but herself."

"Rose said Vava has gone out. It is very naughty of her, isn't it?"

"Very naughty!" Tamara agreed. "I am afraid I shall have to punish her."

"How will you do that?" Kadine asked.

"I will think of something," Tamara answered.

The most effective punishment, she knew, would be to stop Vava from riding, but this was a threat which she did not wish to put into operation unless it was absolutely necessary.

The children were usually so good and so well behaved that there was no need for any punishments.

They had obeyed their father and mother because they loved them, and Tamara knew they obeyed her for the same reason.

At the same time it was naughty of Vava to have gone out early in the morning without telling anyone what she was doing.

Tamara settled Kadine down at the breakfast-table. Then because she felt she could not eat anything herself until she had found Vava she walked through the Castle and out of a door which led almost directly to the stable-yard.

She found a number of stable-boys hurrying about but there was no sign of Vava. Then Tamara saw Abbey coming from one of the stalls.

"Good-morning, Abbey."

"Good-morning, Miss."

"Is Miss Vava here? I am afraid she has played truant and I was sure I would find her with Butterfly."

"No, Miss, her's not been here this morning."

"Are you sure?" Tamara asked.

"Quite sure, Miss. Oi've not seen a sight nor sound o' er."

One of the stable-boys passed as he spoke and he shouted:

"Hi, Bill! Have ye seen anything o' Miss Vava this morn?"

"No, Mr. Abbey."

"Ye're sure her's not been here?"

"Quite sure, Mr. Abbey. Oi've been here since six o'clock."

"She must be somewhere in the Castle," Tamara said and hurried back.

Kadine had finished her breakfast.

"You have been a long time," she remarked, "and I do not want any more."

"Then come and help me find Vava."

Tamara was beginning to feel worried, although she would hardly admit it to herself as they searched everywhere, in the Library, the Salon and even the kitchens.

"Have you seen *Mademoiselle* Vava, *Monsieur*?" Tamara asked the Chef.

"*Mais non, M'mselle*," he replied. Then smiling at Kadine he said:

"If you're a good little girl I'm making you a special cake for tea."

"What sort of cake?" Kadine asked. "Is it a pink one?"

"A pink one with your name on in cherries."

Kadine clapped her hands.

"*Merci, Monsieur! Merci bien!*"

The Chef beamed at her. But Tamara, while amused and glad that he had taken such a liking to the little girls, took Kadine away.

They went up to the Sitting-Room, thinking perhaps Vava had come back but it was empty and Sándor had not seen her either.

Tamara began to get worried.

It was now nearly nine o'clock and she was certain that Vava if nothing else, would be feeling hungry for her breakfast.

114

She was hurrying down the front stairs when she saw the Duke come through the front door.

He had been riding as he usually did early in the morning and was just handing his riding-whip and gloves to one of the footmen when he looked up and saw her.

"Your Grace, we have lost Vava!" Tamara said.

Kadine ran ahead of her down the stairs.

"She has disappeared, Uncle Howard, and she has not had her breakfast. We have searched everywhere. I think a goblin must have spirited her away!"

As she spoke Tamara gave a little cry.

"What is it?" the Duke asked.

"I know where Vava has gone!" she exclaimed. "She has gone to have another look at the gypsy pony! She has not stopped talking about it since she first saw it yesterday."

The Duke frowned.

"I told Melville to get rid of the gypsies."

"They had a piebald foal," Tamara explained, "and Vava was fascinated by it."

"I will go and fetch her back," the Duke said.

"Let me come with you," Tamara pleaded.

The Duke turned to the Butler.

"Order a horse for me, and one for Miss Wynne."

"It will only take me two minutes to change," Tamara said.

She picked up the front of her skirt as she spoke and ran up the stairs.

She ran to her bed-room followed by Kadine.

"You stay here with Sándor," Tamara said.

It literally took her only three minutes to put on her habit. Then she ran back down the stairs to find the Duke outside the front door with two horses.

"I have certainly never known a woman who could change her clothes so quickly!" he said, and to Tamara's surprise he helped her into the saddle.

115

They rode off, galloping the horses over the Park until they came to the far end of it where there was a rough, open piece of ground.

When they reached it Tamara looked at it in consternation.

There were the grey ashes where a fire had burned the night before, there were the marks on the grass of the wheels of caravans, and on one or two bramble bushes there were a few colourful rags which had obviously been discarded, but otherwise there was no sign of the gypsies.

"They have gone!" she exclaimed.

She turned to look at the Duke.

"You turned them away," she said. "Do you think they have taken Vava with them?

CHAPTER SIX

There was a throb in Tamara's voice as she spoke. Then the Duke said:

"They will not have gone far and we will follow them."

He moved his horse ahead as he spoke.

They crossed the road which formed the boundary of the Park, and now stretching over the countryside there were thick almost impenetrable woods.

Tamara was suddenly afraid that once the gypsies disappeared among the dark trees it would be impossible for an outsider to find them.

She was aware that the gypsies had secret paths by which they moved from place to place, but she hardly expected the Duke would know of them.

Yet he rode confidently ahead and after twisting between the trees they came upon a narrow track which was just wide enough, Tamara realised, for a Caravan.

She saw there were deep ruts made by wheels, but at the same time they could have been made by the carts used by the wood-cutters.

The Duke went on without hesitating. Although she longed to ask him where he was going and if he was certain they were moving in the right direction, she felt as if her throat was constricted.

All she could think of was Vava being carried away by the gypsies to some unknown destination where they would never find her again.

There were always stories circulating among villagers about the gypsies. How they not only stole eggs and chickens, ducks and small lambs, but also children.

In the past Tamara had never believed such tales, thinking that the gypsies had so many children of their own that they were unlikely to want anyone else's.

But now the stories which had been repeated and repeated for generations amongst illiterate people, who were afraid of the gypsies' curse or the 'evil eye', came flooding back into her mind.

They made her feel more and more afraid with every pace her horse took.

Then unexpectedly there was a clearing deep in the wood and she saw that it must have been used as a camping-ground for years.

There were the grey ashes of a dozen fires and again fluttering, colourful rags on bushes and low branches of the trees – but there were no gypsies.

Even as Tamara parted her lips to ask the Duke what they should do now, she saw Vava.

The child came running towards them from the shadow of a fir tree.

"Vava!" Tamara exclaimed.

The Duke turned back to take her horse's bridle and she slipped from the saddle onto the ground to run towards Vava, her arms outstretched.

"Oh, Aunt Tamara! I'se frightened!" Vava cried.

Then as Tamara's arms went round her she burst into tears.

Tamara knelt down on the ground and held her close.

"It is all right, darling," she said soothingly. "We have found you and you are quite safe now."

"The gypsies left me . . . alone," Vava sobbed. "They said I was to . . . stay here and not to . . . run away . . . but I was . . . frightened all by . . . myself."

"I am here now," Tamara said. "The Duke and I will take you home. We have been searching for you everywhere."

She wiped away Vava's tears and, picking her up in her arms, she walked back towards her horse.

"I will take her in front of my saddle," the Duke said.

As Tamara hesitated he said to Vava:

"I am sure you would like to ride on Samson."

Vava's dark eye-lashes were still wet, but now she smiled.

She held up her arms to the Duke and he took her from Tamara and set her on his saddle in front of him.

"Can you manage to mount by yourself?" he asked Tamara.

"I have managed to do so for a great number of years," she answered.

But she too was smiling. It was so wonderful to have found Vava safe and sound!

They turned their horses' heads back in the direction from which they had come.

"I went to look for the little piebald pony," Vava explained, "and the gypsy lady said I was to go with them."

"You should not have gone out alone so early in the morning," Tamara said.

But it was difficult to make her voice sound severe, she was so glad to have Vava back again.

"I wanted to see the pony," Vava said. Then looking up at the Duke she added: "The gypsies were very angry with you, Uncle Howard, because you turned them away."

There was a pause, before the Duke replied:

"I will tell you what we will do, Vava. This afternoon, if you are not too tired, or to-morrow morning, we will go to the entrance to the Park and look for the signs left by the gypsies for other gypsies who may want to camp there."

"What sort of signs?" Vava asked.

"They have one which means: 'Nice people – can camp

119

here'," the Duke answered, "and another which says: 'These people do not like gypsies'."

Vava considered this for a moment, then she said:

"As you turned them away, that is the sign they will have left behind."

"Exactly!" the Duke agreed, "and that is why you and I will alter it. Then other gypsies will come and you will be able to see their piebald ponies if they have any."

"I would like that," Vava cried.

"But you are never to go there without me," Tamara interrupted quickly. "You know that was very naughty."

"I am . . . sorry," Vava said.

But her voice was no longer frightened as she leaned back comfortably against the Duke, putting her hands on the reins in front of his.

"I am riding Samson," she said proudly, "just like Sándor did."

"Samson is really too big for Sándor," the Duke answered, "and you will have to grow very much bigger before you can ride him."

"When I am grown up I shall take him over the jumps," Vava said confidently.

"By the time you are grown up Samson may be too old," the Duke replied with a smile.

Listening to him talk to Vava, Tamara thought she would never have imagined he could be so kind or so understanding to a child.

Now for the first time since leaving the Castle, too agitated to think of anything but Vava, she thought how handsome he was and how magnificent he looked on the big black stallion.

She found herself glancing at his clear-cut features, the way he rode as if he seemed part of the horse itself.

She thought too that the lines of cynicism at the sides of his mouth seemed lighter and there was a twinkle in his eyes

120

she had not noticed before.

When they reached the Park Vava wished to go faster and to please her the Duke put Samson into a trot and Tamara did the same with her horse.

When they had nearly reached the Castle she said:

"Can we go straight into the stable-yard? I know how worried Abbey was at Vava's disappearance and I am sure that he will want to know we have found her."

The Duke did not reply, he merely smiled at her. Then as they rode over the cobble-stones of the stable-yard Abbey came hurrying out of a stall exclaiming in delight:

"Ye've found Miss Vava, Your Grace! It's thankful Oi am that she's safely home again."

"Quite safe, Abbey," the Duke replied.

The old groom reached up to take Vava from the saddle but she screamed:

"No! I want to ride Samson over the jumps. Please, Uncle Howard, let me ride him round the race-course."

"I am afraid you would find it difficult to keep in the saddle if I did that," the Duke answered, "but I will tell you what I will do, I will jump Samson over the five-bar gate, and you can come and watch."

"All right," Vava agreed.

She let Abbey lift her to the ground, then Tamara also dismounted and they walked hand-in-hand to the end of the stables.

The Duke took Samson back a little way, then put him at the gate and the horse went forward confidently.

It was a jump he had done dozens of times, but as he nearly reached it Tamara suddenly thought that the gate seemed higher than she remembered.

As the horse took off she thought how graceful the animal looked and how superbly the Duke was riding him.

Then there was the sound of Samson's front hoofs hitting the top bar, a sharp crack which seemed almost like the report of a pistol, and to Tamara's horror and the consternation of Abbey, who gave a hoarse cry, the gate did not give way.

Samson fell and, as he collapsed onto his knees, the Duke was shot over his head to fall heavily to the ground.

It was Tamara who reached him first and as she bent down to touch him she saw that his eyes were closed.

With a sudden fear which seemed to strike her almost like a dagger in her heart, she thought he was dead.

Tamara walked along the passage from the West Wing and as she reached the Grand Staircase she saw two men going down it, their voices low as they talked to each other.

She knew that one of them was the local doctor who had been sent for as soon as the Duke had been carried back to the Castle on an improvised stretcher. The other was the Specialist who had arrived from London a few hours ago.

Yesterday after the accident the Duke had remained unconscious and Tamara had enquired after him nearly every hour, but Watkins could tell her very little.

First thing this morning she had learnt that the Duke had regained consciousness but was in great pain.

"I've never known anything like it, Miss," Watkins said shaking his head. "It seems as if the Master's in agony, and it's not like him to complain unless it's real bad."

"Surely there is something the doctor can give him so that he need not suffer unnecessarily?" Tamara asked.

"Dr. Emmerton is waiting the arrival of Sir George Seymour from London, Miss," Watkins explained. "He's the King's doctor, you know, and one can't ask for better."

"Yes, I am sure Dr. Emmerton is right," Tamara said reflectively. "It would be a mistake to do anything of which Sir George might not approve."

At the same time it hurt her in a manner she could not understand to think that the Duke was suffering.

Watkins had said he was very ill, and she could remember all too vividly her feelings when she saw him lying on the ground and thought he was dead.

It had been agony too to watch the men lift him and carry him back to the Castle and know that he was unconscious of what was happening.

Only a little while earlier she had been thinking how magnificent he looked on Samson, and now like a great oak fallen to the ground he was helpless and still.

To look at him made her feel curiously near to tears.

She had been unable to sleep all night for thinking of him, and even the fact that Sándor was much better and, having eaten a large breakfast demanded to get up, could not erase her feeling of depression.

There was also at the back of her mind the problem of the five-bar gate.

When she had risen from the Duke's side to allow the men to lift him onto the stretcher to take him back to the Castle, she had turned to look at the gate and wondered why it had not fallen as it should have done.

Then she saw that it had in fact been nailed firmly to the posts on either side of it.

What was more she saw that her first impression had been correct and the gate was some five inches higher than it had been when it swung lightly as the Duke had designed it.

"Who could have done such a thing?" she asked.

She knew without being told that it was someone on the Estate, some employee who hated his Master and had planned to take his revenge as other labourers were trying to do all over the country.

Even while she admitted that it had perhaps been the Duke's fault, she knew that personally whatever he had done she could not bear to see him punished in such a way.

She had been waiting all the morning to hear Sir George's verdict and now as she reached the Duke's bed-room and was just about to knock, the door opened and Watkins came out.

"I came to enquire . . ." Tamara began, then her voice died away.

The old valet was crying, the tears running down his cheeks.

"What is it?" she asked in a whisper.

"It's the Master, Miss."

Tamara drew in her breath.

"He is not . . . dead?" she could hardly say the words.

Then even as she uttered them little above a whisper she knew as her heart seemed to contract that she loved him.

The knowledge was so overwhelming, at the same time so painful, that she could only stand feeling as if she was turned to stone.

Watkins, wiping his eyes with the back of his hand, said: "No, Miss not dead, worse!"

"What could be . . . worse?" Tamara asked still in a whisper because the words could hardly pass her lips.

"Sir George says that the Master's broken his back, Miss, and he'll always be paralysed!"

As if it was too much to bear, Watkins covered his eyes with his hand.

Tamara stood staring at him, the colour fading from her cheeks leaving her very pale.

"It cannot be . . . true! Is Sir George . . . certain?"

"He's bringing another Specialist down to-morrow, Miss, but I knows by the way he spoke and the expression on Dr. Emmerton's face they didn't think there's much hope."

There was a pause when Tamara was unable to speak before Watkins said:

"The Master'd rather be dead and gone than have to put up with such a life, I knows that!"

Tamara was sure of it too.

But because she felt the conflicting emotions within her

had sapped her power of thought she could only stand staring at Watkins' wet face.

"There must be something we can do," she said frantically after some moments had passed.

"Dr. Emmerton's sending his carriage back with something to relieve His Grace's pain," Watkins said. "But he's lying there a-swearing he'll not take their damned drugs! He's never had any use for them."

Tamara did not speak and Watkins went on:

"It's terrible to see him, Miss – terrible!"

Tamara felt her fingers were clenched together. Then as she longed to do something, yearned as she had never yearned in her whole life before to be able to help, she felt as if she faced an insurmountable barrier.

She only stood immobile.

Watkins drew a crumpled handkerchief from his pocket and wiped his face with it.

"I must get back to His Grace, Miss."

He turned towards the door and as he did so a footman came along the passage.

"I was a-looking for you, Miss," he said to Tamara. "There's a man at the back-door as wishes to speak to you."

"A man?" Tamara asked, finding it difficult to concentrate on what the footman was saying.

"Yes, Miss, he says he comes from Cornwall and you'd be expecting him. He be blind."

Tamara gave a little cry.

"It is Erth! Erth Veryon! Where is he? Take me to him quickly!"

The footman glanced at her in surprise and led the way down the back stairs to the kitchen door.

Standing outside, his white hair blowing in the warm breeze was Erth Veryon and beside him stood his grandson.

"Erth! Erth!" Tamara cried putting out her hands towards him. "You have come at exactly the right moment! I need you – I need you desperately!"

"The Lord guided me here," Erth said in his deep voice with its Cornish accent. "I felt there was work for me to do."

"There is indeed," Tamara said. "Come upstairs. Come and see the Duke. He has had a fall . . . a terrible fall from his horse . . . and the doctors say that he has broken his back and will be paralysed!"

She took Erth's hand in hers as she spoke and drew him along the flagged passage which led to the kitchen door.

As she touched him she felt that strange vibration that she had felt before when he had held her hand in farewell.

They walked up the stairs.

Even as they went some part of Tamara's mind questioned whether Erth would be able to do anything for the Duke, when the King's doctor had said it was hopeless.

And yet she had seen his wonderful healing powers on her brother-in-law and on the people in the village at home.

She knew too that his reputation was so great that the fisher-folk and the villagers all over Cornwall looked on him almost as a Saint.

"Send for Erth!" was a cry that went up when anyone was injured or so ill that they had been given up by the Physicians.

Only as Tamara reached the landing outside the Duke's bed-room did she wonder what he would think if she brought him a blind healer.

She could not help feeling that he might dismiss anything so controversial as such healing as being nonsense and would perhaps refuse to allow Erth to help him.

For a moment she was afraid, but as if he knew what she was thinking Erth said quietly:

"You have to trust in God, child, and His love. It never fails."

Tamara drew in her breath.

"I trust you, Erth," she said quietly and knocked on the

126

Duke's door.

Watkins opened it and looked surprised when he saw there was a man with Tamara.

"I wish to speak to His Grace," Tamara said.

She walked forward, still leading Erth by the hand.

She had never been in the Duke's bed-room before and she had an impression of a huge high-ceilinged room that was as magnificent as its owner.

There were curtains of ruby red velvet not only at the windows but also at the sides of the great canopied bed which reached almost to the ceiling.

The family coat-of-arms was embroidered above the Duke's head and he was lying flat on his back so that he gave the impression, Tamara thought, of a stone figure on top of a tomb.

She forced the thought from her mind and went forward still drawing Erth with her until she stood beside the bed.

The Duke's eyes were closed but she could see that he was in pain by the frown on his forehead and the way his lips were pressed together as if to prevent him from crying out loud.

"Your . . . Grace!"

Tamara's voice was hardly above a whisper but he heard it and his eyes opened.

He looked at her not in surprise, she thought, but as if in a dull agony he appealed to her for help, yet knew she could not give it to him.

"Your Grace!" Tamara said again. "I have brought you a man who will heal you."

The Duke's expression did not alter and she went on:

"He healed your brother, Lord Ronald, and in Cornwall we all believed there that he has a power which is not of this world. Will you please let him help you?"

For one moment she thought the Duke was about to refuse. Then he said in a voice which was little more than a croak:

127

"If he can – take this damned – pain away I will – believe anything you tell me about – him."

Tamara felt a sudden lightness within her because she had been so afraid . . . so desperately afraid that the Duke would refuse to have anything to do with Erth.

Now she stood aside and the blind man went to the bed.

Tamara moved back against the wall, while Erth's grandson and Watkins stood just inside the door.

Erth stood straight and still beside the Duke and Tamara knew, for she had learnt in Cornwall how he worked, that he was seeing the patient's aura and finding out where the damage lay.

He stood without moving for nearly a minute.

Tamara held her breath waiting and praying wordlessly in her heart that the Duke could be healed.

Then at last Erth moved and very gently he slipped his hand under the Duke's body just below his shoulder.

He moved the sheets as he did so and Tamara realised that because the Duke had been examined by the doctors he was not wearing a night-shirt but was in bed naked.

Gentle though Erth was, the Duke gave a murmur of pain and the Healer spoke for the first time.

"It'll be better in a short while," he said quietly. "The pain'll go."

As he spoke he laid his other hand on the Duke's chest and this Tamara knew was the moment when the power which Erth believed came from God passed from him into the injured person's body.

Erth raised his head a little, almost as if he was looking up into the Heavens.

Tamara knew he was praying and that he spoke with God and asked Him to heal through His love the man whose body was broken.

There was complete silence in the room for several minutes. Then the Duke said:

"I can feel a strange throbbing and an intense heat. It seems to come from your hands."

Erth did not reply and after a moment the Duke said in a different tone:

"The pain is going – in fact it has gone!"

Tamara clasped her hands together.

Now for the first time the tears came into her eyes, tears of relief and happiness. As she felt them she knew how much she loved the Duke.

It seemed absurd that she should love him considering how violently she had hated him, and yet there was no mistaking the ecstasy within her heart.

She had loved him, she thought, long before she had acknowledged it herself when Watkins told her that he was paralysed.

Love had come to her so insidiously and so slowly that she had not recognised it.

She had only known it had been impossible for her not to keep thinking of the Duke. In fact even when she hated him he filled her mind to the exclusion of all else.

Then when he had been so kind to Sándor, when he had apologised to the boy for sending him to the wrong school, she had known, as Sándor had said, that he was big – big enough to acknowledge he had made a mistake.

That was something that few men in his position would have been prepared to do.

It was perhaps then, she thought, that everything she had felt about him had changed.

From that moment every minute, every hour, she had fallen deeper in love with him even though she would not admit it to herself.

The pain she had experienced when she saw him fall from Samson should have told her, but she had been too numb with shock.

It was only Watkins' announcement of what the doctors

had said which had made her know the truth almost as if it had been written in letters of fire upon her heart.

'I love him!' she thought now. 'I love everything about him: his magnificence, his kindness to Vava, the way he understood what I was feeling when she was lost.'

It all flashed through her mind as she waited, tense in the quiet room to see if Erth could perform what would be a miracle.

"The throbbing and the heat are going now," the Duke said after what seemed a long time.

Erth turned his head downwards almost as if he could see. Then he said, a smile on his lips:

"Will Your Grace move your arm?"

"I – cannot do – so . . ." the Duke began.

But as he spoke he moved his left arm from his side straight out to shoulder level.

"Now your right," Erth said quietly.

The Duke did as he was told.

Then as the full significance of what had happened came to him he said in a low voice, deeply moved with emotion:

"You have healed me!"

"It is God who has done that," Erth answered, "not I."

"What can I say?" the Duke asked.

"Just give thanks to God who loves and cares for His children and allows me, His servant, if it is His will, to help them."

"I can move! I am not paralysed!" The Duke said and the words sounded as if he could hardly believe them to be true.

He would have sat up, but Erth's hand was on his shoulder.

"Lie still, Your Grace," he said. "Your back will ache a little to-day and perhaps to-morrow, but let the power of God work slowly – slowly!"

He repeated the word with a smile. Then he turned from the bed and Tamara, knowing what he wanted, went towards

130

him and took his hand in hers.

"How can I thank you?" she asked.

"I want no thanks," Erth answered. "I came because you needed me."

"The children will want to see you."

"Then take me to them."

"After you have seen them please do not leave," the Duke said. "I would like you to stay at least until to-morrow in case I have a relapse."

"You will not need me again, Your Grace," Erth replied, "and my grandson and I must be on our way."

"I want to offer you my hospitality for as long as you wish," the Duke said.

"I am needed to the north of where I am now," Erth said quietly, almost as if he heard someone telling him so.

"Then what can I do to express my gratitude?" the Duke asked.

Erth did not answer. He was moving across the room towards his grandson.

Tamara went to the Duke's side.

"Give him anything he wants," the Duke ordered.

"He will take no money," Tamara answered, "but I will see what I can do for him."

The Duke's eyes were looking into hers.

"Thank you," he said quietly.

Because she was afraid he would read in her face what she felt about him, she turned quickly away.

She took Erth to their Sitting-Room in the West Wing and Sándor greeted him with an exclamation of surprise that was almost a shout.

"Erth! What are you doing here?"

"Erth has healed the Duke," Tamara explained.

"If you had come yesterday you could have healed me!"

"What have you been doing to yourself, Master Sándor?" Erth asked.

131

He put out his hand as he spoke and laid it unerringly on Sándor's bruised eye.

"It is all right, Erth," Sándor said uncomfortably.

"Stand still," Tamara ordered. "You know Erth will make it better."

"He is making it tingle," Sándor complained.

Erth paid no attention. He merely kept his hand over the bruised eye then with the other touched Sándor's split lip.

After a moment Sándor's somewhat embarrassed protests died away and he stood still.

When Erth finally took his hands from him he said:

"You are jolly good at this sort of thing, Erth! My eye feels much better already!"

The blind man put his hands on his shoulders.

"I will take away the stiffness," he said. "Your body is bruised but there is no real harm done."

"If you do that I shall be able to ride," Sándor said suddenly in a different tone.

Erth smiled.

"You'll ride to-morrow, Master Sándor, and the bruises 'll fade."

"How do you know I have bruises . . . ?" Sándor began, then looking at Tamara grinned. "He is a wizard!"

"I think that is the right word," Tamara smiled.

She was so happy about the Duke that she almost felt she could dance on air.

She longed to go back to his room to talk to him, to make quite certain that his recovery was permanent.

Instead she ordered food for Erth and his grandson. When they were leaving she slipped some golden sovereigns into the boy's hand.

She offered him five, but he shook his head and took only one.

She knew she could not argue with him and he was taking only enough to take care of his grandfather on his travels.

For reasons of his own Erth would not possess any worldly goods.

Erth saw Kadine and Vava, and as they all escorted him to the front door to say good-bye he took Tamara's hand in his and said:

"The poison has gone. You no longer hate, my child, but love. That's good! Now you'll find happiness."

Tamara looked at him in a startled manner and because the children were listening she did not reply. She only bent her head and kissed Erth's hand.

Smiling as if he understood why she thanked him, he and his grandson set off down the drive and Tamara watched them until they were nearly out of sight.

They went upstairs to the Sitting room and Tamara read to Kadine and Vava until it was time for them to go to bed.

"I can dine downstairs with you to-night," Sándor said to Tamara. "You heard Erth say I will be able to ride to-morrow?"

"I heard that," Tamara answered, "and you will also be well enough to do lessons."

"That is unfair!" Sándor said. "You said I need not do any until the end of the week."

"If you are well enough to ride you are also well enough to do a certain amount of mathematics," Tamara said severely.

Sándor made a little grimace, but he did not go on protesting and after a moment he asked:

"Why did Erth come here?"

"He said he knew that we needed him."

"He really has cured Uncle Howard?"

Tamara nodded.

She had not told Sándor that the Duke had been paralysed.

Now she thought to herself how incredible it was that if Erth had not appeared he would have been obliged to lie there immobile and perhaps later only move about in a wheel-chair.

"Thank you, God, thank you," she said in her heart.

Then even as she prayed in gratitude she found a question asking itself in her mind:

"What will it mean to you?" and was afraid of the answer.

Tamara came downstairs having left Kadine and Vava in Rose's charge while they rested after luncheon.

Sándor had ridden in the morning and she had insisted on his resting in the afternoon.

Although he made a feeble protest she felt he was in fact rather tired and quite prepared without much persuasion to ie on the sofa and read a book.

Tamara was going to the Library to find a book for herself.

So much had happened in the last few days that she had felt unable to read.

Only now when she decided to sit down quietly with a book for an hour did she find she had finished the two books she had taken from the Library and must therefore change them for others.

She had learnt from Watkins that the Duke had had a good night and was thinking of getting up.

"Please persuade His Grace to rest a little longer," she said to Watkins, wishing she could say it to the Duke herself.

"You know Erth Veryon said he would feel sore for a little while."

"It's very different, Miss, feeling sore an' being unable t' move," Watkins replied.

"I know," Tamara said, "but His Grace would be wise to take things quietly for the rest of the week."

The valet chuckled.

"You'll have to talk to him, Miss. His Grace won't listen to me and he resents being 'mollycoddled' as he calls it."

"I can understand that," Tamara said, "but try and persuade him to be sensible."

She thought that perhaps she would be able to see the Duke during the evening as she had a feeling that he might come downstairs for dinner.

She was therefore surprised when she reached the Hall and was just about to go along the corridor towards the Library when a footman came from the Blue Salon to say:

"His Grace wishes to speak to you, Miss."

"He is downstairs?" Tamara queried.

"His Grace came down for luncheon, Miss."

The footman opened the door and Tamara went in.

The Duke was sitting in an arm-chair by one of the windows.

When she entered he rose to his feet.

"Please do not get up!" she begged, moving quickly across the room, her eyes on his face.

He was looking magnificent as he always did and even more handsome than she remembered.

She thought, too, that he looked happy: there were no longer the lines of pain on his face, nor were there any of cynicism.

There was a faint smile on his lips as he watched her coming towards him. When she reached his side and looked up, there was an expression in his eyes that made her heart give a sudden leap.

"I have a lot to say to you," he said quietly, "and I must begin by thanking you for saving my life."

"It was Erth who did that."

"But you brought him to me, and I gather that in some strange way which I cannot understand he knew that he would be needed here."

"He was needed," Tamara said. "He has made you well again."

"I can hardly believe it," the Duke answered, "and as I have said I have to thank you."

"You are making me feel embarrassed," Tamara protested. "We are all so grateful and so very, very happy that you are well again."

The Duke raised his eye-brows.

"We?"

"Everybody in the household."

"You are sure of that?"

"But of course!" she answered, a little embarrassed by his probing.

"I am waiting for you to tell me it was my own fault that the accident happened."

She looked at him in surprise, then he indicated a chair opposite his own.

"Suppose we sit down?" he suggested. "I think we have a lot to discuss with each other."

Tamara sat down with a look of apprehension in her eyes as she raised them to the Duke's.

"It was intended I should have that fall," the Duke said. "I have since learnt that not only was the gate firmly fixed to the posts, but it had also been raised to a height which made it impossible for almost any horse to jump it without falling."

"Who could have done such a thing?" Tamara asked.

The Duke shrugged his shoulders.

"Any number of difficult people who are dissatisfied with the conditions on this Estate."

"What are you going to do about it?"

She thought as she spoke it was perhaps presumptuous of her to ask the question.

"Change the conditions!" the Duke answered. "That surely is what you would advise me to do?"

"I gather there is unrest here, as there is in many other parts of the country," Tamara said. "I think the working people need sympathy and understanding and somebody to listen to their complaints."

"That is exactly what I intend to do," the Duke answered,

"so you see, our minds are thinking along the same lines."

He smiled as he spoke and she felt as if her heart moved in her breast towards him.

"And now," the Duke said, "suppose we discuss our nephew and nieces?"

Tamara's eyes opened wide and the colour rose in her cheeks.

"You can hardly go on pretending," the Duke said quietly.

"You . . . heard Vava call me . . . Aunt Tamara."

"I had rather suspected the truth before I had that confirmation of it," the Duke answered. "I could not believe any disinterested Governess would have been quite so passionately concerned for her charges."

Tamara dropped her eyes and her eye-lashes were very dark against her white skin.

"I . . . I thought you would not . . . accept me here if you knew I was . . . Maïka's sister," she murmured a little incoherently.

"I have an explanation about that which I would wish you to listen to," the Duke said. "You see, Tamara, I want you to understand my behaviour towards my brother."

She looked up at him when he used her Christian name and her eyes were on his face as he went on:

"When my brother Ronald married I was not in this country and had no knowledge of my father's attitude until some years later."

As if he realised Tamara's surprise he explained:

"In August 1808 I landed in Portugal under the command of Sir Arthur Wellesley."

"You were with your Regiment?"

"Yes, we were fighting the French on the Peninsula, and as you are well aware it was a long-drawn-out campaign."

"So you did not know your brother had married?"

"I had not the least idea of it, for as you can imagine letters from home, if they were written, seldom arrived on the battle-field."

"I can understand that," Tamara murmured.

She was beginning, she thought, to understand other things as well.

"It was not until I returned home after the war was over that I learnt from my father what had occurred."

"Why did you not then get in touch with Lord Ronald?"

"I wanted to do so, but my father, who was still furiously angry with him for having married against his wishes, declared that he had no knowledge of his whereabouts, and although I made several enquiries no-one else seemed to have any idea where he could be."

"But his allowance . . . ?"

"I was coming to that," the Duke answered. "It was not until my father died and I inherited that I discovered that despite my father's antipathy Ronald had been paid an allowance all through the years. I continued it, but I made no further effort towards a reconciliation."

"Why not?" Tamara asked.

The Duke looked away from her out of the window.

"This is hard to explain," he said. "I do not know if Ronald ever told you what our lives were like when we were boys."

"I gathered that your father and mother did not give you very much love or understanding."

"I think they disliked us," the Duke said. "We were relegated to the care of servants. The only times I can remember my father speaking to me was when he was punishing me for some misdeed or other."

He paused as if the memories of his miserable childhood were painful to recall. Then he went on:

"We were both of us much happier at school than we were at home, and I enjoyed the Army because it gave me the companionship and I suppose a sense of purpose I had never had before."

138

The Duke's voice sharpened as he went on:

"But it was a hard life and a very tough one. I would want no son of mine to see the sights I saw, to endure the horrors of a battle-field or to hear the cries of the wounded and dying."

Tamara drew in her breath.

She had never expected to hear the Duke speak in such a manner or to feel so deeply about the sufferings of other people.

"I came back to England," the Duke went on in a different tone, "determined to make up for the gaiety I had missed through being continually at war. I went to London."

There was a faint, mocking smile on his lips as he said:

"You are too young to understand what London seemed like to me after being in Europe for so long."

"It . . . shocked you?" Tamara asked.

She remembered the stories she had heard of the promiscuity, the raffishness and the extravagance of the Rakes and Dandies.

"I was shocked at the indifference and callousness shown towards the men who had fought and died for the freedom of this country," the Duke replied. "I suppose you might say it made me very cynical and disillusioned."

He paused before he said:

"I was also disillusioned where women were concerned, but that is something which need not concern you."

Tamara felt a little stab of jealousy.

Women, she was quite sure, would have found him irresistible, and perhaps he had found them alluring and very desirable after spending so many years almost entirely in the company of men.

"When I inherited the title," the Duke said, "I came back here thinking that perhaps my father's way of life and his indifference to other people's feelings was better than being emotionally involved in situations one could not help."

139

He paused.

"I did not wish to be hurt as I had been hurt as a child by the coldness and indifference of my parents. I told myself that I did not need love, that I could manage very well without love in my life."

Then looking at Tamara he said very quietly:

"I was wrong! I cannot do without it any longer!"

Her eyes met his and for a moment she could not move, until hardly knowing what she was doing she rose to her feet and moved closer to the window.

She heard the Duke rise too. Then he was standing a little behind her and so close that she felt herself tremble.

"You know what I am trying to say to you, Tamara," he said. "I think I have loved you since the moment I saw you with your eyes blazing hatred at me, and yet I knew you were what I had been seeking all my life!"

Tamara made what tried to be a little murmur of protest, but the Duke's arms were round her.

He pulled her against him, and before she realised what was happening his lips were on hers.

For a moment she was still in surprise, then she felt a sudden rapture so wonderful, so glorious, that she knew that this too, was what she had been seeking and yet had not been aware of it.

He held her closer and still closer and the pressure of his lips deepened on hers until she felt as if he drew her heart from her body and made it his.

She had never been kissed before, she had no idea that such a sensation of wonder and ecstasy could be transmitted from one mouth to another.

Yet it was everything she had always longed for, so beautiful, so spiritual that it was part of the divine, and she felt as if her whole body became alive.

The Duke raised his head.

"I love you, my darling, I love you more than I can begin

to tell you!"

"I . . . love you!" Tamara whispered.

Then he was kissing her again, wildly, frantically, as if he was afraid of losing her and must make sure she was his and she could not escape him.

Now it seemed to Tamara that his kisses awoke a flame within her, flickering at first until it seemed to grow, burning its way from her heart, through her breast to her lips, to be ignited with the flame that was burning in him.

"You are so perfect, so sweet, unspoilt and innocent," the Duke said hoarsely. "Oh, my darling, there is no-one like you."

Then even as he spoke Tamara remembered.

She felt as if an icy hand gripped at her heart and with a little cry her fingers went up to her lips.

Then wrenching herself from the Duke's arms she turned and ran away from him across the room.

She pulled open the door and still running tore up the staircase, tears gathering in her eyes and in her throat until they were choking her.

As she reached the West Wing she tore into her bed-room and shut the door behind her.

Standing in the centre of the room her hands went up to her face covering her eyes.

"Oh, God, Oh, God!" she cried. "How can I tell him?"

CHAPTER SEVEN

Tamara stood for some moments with her hands over her eyes. Then as if she made up her mind she rushed to the cupboard in the corner of the room and pulled out a leather round-topped trunk.

She opened it and started to open the drawers of the chest, packing the first things that came to hand.

She was kneeling on the floor in front of the trunk when she heard the door open.

"I am busy!" she said, thinking it would be Rose.

The door shut and she thought whoever it was who had come to find her had gone. Then a voice asked:

"What do you think you are doing?"

She started violently, turned her head and saw it was the Duke who was standing in her room.

She only glanced at him for a moment, then she looked back again into the trunk, still kneeling, her head bent, the sunshine pouring in through the window glinting on her red hair.

"I am . . . going . . . away."

It was difficult to hear the words, and yet she had said them.

"Why?"

The monosyllable seemed to echo round the room, and as she did not answer she heard the Duke cross the carpet to stand nearer to her while she still had her back to him.

"If you go away," he asked after a moment, "what will become of the children?"

"They will be ... all right with you ... now," Tamara answered.

And yet at the thought of leaving them she felt the tears come into her eyes and begin to run down her face.

She thought that if she kept her head bent he would not realise she was crying and after a moment he said:

"Can you really relinquish your responsibilities so easily?"

There was silence, until he added reflectively, almost as if he was talking to himself:

"You fought so hard and so valiantly for what you believed was right for them. If you leave them now they will lack the most important thing of all – your love."

It flashed through Tamara's mind how strange it was to hear him speaking in such a way.

How could she have imagined when first she came to the Castle that the autocratic, overwhelming Duke of Granchester would ever speak to her of love?

Or even more extraordinary, that he would kiss her and she would feel as if he was lifting her up into the sky?

She would never know such rapture or wonder again, she told herself despairingly, but she could not stay and deceive him.

Worst of all she could not tell him the truth and know that what he would feel for her was contempt and disgust.

"I do not understand what has upset you," the Duke said. "Could we not talk it over together, you and I, Tamara?"

It was the hardest thing she had ever done, Tamara thought, to resist him when he talked in such a beguiling manner.

She had loved him, she thought, because he was so magnificent and because it was impossible to compare him with any other man she had ever seen or known.

She had known when he told her how he had suffered as a

143

boy and how disillusioned he had been when he returned from the war, that she loved him with tenderness and compassion and she longed to comfort him.

But now she found him irresistible and she loved him in yet another way.

"I thought for one magical moment that your hate for me had gone," the Duke said in a low voice. "You said you loved me, and I believed you."

"I do . . . love you!"

Tamara felt the words come between her lips without her conscious volition.

"Then why, my darling, are you leaving me?"

"I . . . have to."

"You must give me a reason."

"I cannot do that. Please . . . please let me go."

"And if I refuse?"

Tamara bent her head a little lower and now the tears were falling from her eyes into the trunk.

They splashed down onto some of the garments she had already packed, but still she made no effort to wipe them away. She only wished she could sink into the ground and be swallowed up by quicksand so that the Duke could never find her again.

She heard him walk to the window to stand looking out onto the lake. After a moment he said:

"All my life I have known there was something wrong with the Castle. It is splendid in its own way, and I am not boasting when I say that its surroundings are more beautiful than you would find anywhere else in the whole length and breadth of England."

Tamara made a little sound, which might have been an expression of agreement.

"But I always knew there was something missing," the Duke went on. "As a child I remember it being very cold, and except when Ronald was there I think I always felt lonely and out of touch with the rest of the world."

There was a note in his voice which moved Tamara deeply.

"When I inherited the title and decided to live here," he continued, "I think the Castle itself made me more reserved, more introvert, than I was already. It was almost as if my father's shadow with his oppression and inhibitions enveloped me. I began to be like him both in character and personality."

"I am sure that is . . . not true," Tamara murmured.

"I think it is," the Duke replied. "In fact I am sure that I was becoming as cold, disdainful and harsh as my father was. Then everything changed!"

A new note came into his voice as he went on:

"You appeared unexpectedly, unheralded, and when I walked into the room and saw you there something inside me which I did not even know existed came to life."

He gave a short laugh.

"I did not acknowledge it at the time. I told myself that you were far too beautiful to be trustworthy, and I suspected that you were not what you purported to be."

Tamara thought, although she did not turn her head, that he looked at her before he said with a hint of amusement in his tone:

"I was right, and let me tell you, my darling, that no woman in her senses would engage as a Governess anyone so lovely as you. It would be far too dangerous for her peace of mind."

Again there was the new note of warmth in the Duke's tone.

Tamara felt her tears falling faster and because she was afraid that she would break down all together and lie sobbing at his feet, she clenched her hands until the knuckles showed white on the leather sides of her trunk.

"Every day you seemed to creep further and further into my heart," the Duke went on. "I found myself counting the

145

hours until I could see you. When I left the house I had to force myself to do so because I was afraid of the emotions you aroused in me."

There was no doubt he was smiling as he continued:

"You do not know how many sleepless nights I passed lying awake thinking of you, wanting you, and yet aware that you hated me."

"How . . . were you . . . sure of that?" Tamara asked as if she could not help the question.

"If I had not heard it in your voice and the way you spoke to me, I could see it in your eyes," the Duke said. "I do not think any woman could have more expressive or indeed more beautiful eyes."

He paused before he added softly:

"But when I looked at them as I lay paralysed, they told me that you were feeling something very different."

He was silent for a moment before he said again in that beguiling tone that Tamara found so hard to resist:

"I thought then that you cared for me a little, and when you came into the Blue Salon just now I was sure I saw love in your eyes."

Tamara did not speak and he said:

"Was I wrong? Oh, my darling, do not torture me – tell me I was not wrong."

There was a pregnant silence and Tamara longed to rise to her feet and run to his arms. Then she knew that because she loved him so desperately she could not at the same time deceive him.

She knew the Duke was waiting and after a moment she said, the tears making her voice almost incoherent:

"I . . . love you . . . but I have to . . . go away."

"Why?" the Duke asked as he had asked before.

"I . . . I . . . cannot tell you . . ."

"You have to tell me. Can you imagine what it would be like if you leave me here tortured with questions I cannot answer, wondering which of my many faults has driven you away?"

"No ... no," Tamara cried qu ickly. "It is not ...your fault that I am ... leaving ... it is mine ... only ... m . mine."

"Your fault?" The Duke asked. "What can you have done, my precious? What possible crime can you have committed that you will not tell me?"

She knew he was supposing she must have some quite unimportant reason for making the decision she had.

"Please ... will you try to ... understand?" she begged after a moment. "It ... it is best for you not to ... know only let me assure you that it is ... nothing you have said or done ... but something which only concerns ... myself."

"Come here, Tamara!"

She shook her head.

"I want you to come to me."

"Please ... leave me alone," she cried, "if you ... l.love me just make it easy for me to ... go away ... then forget m.me."

"Do you really believe that is possible?" he enquired. "I am not a boy, Tamara, who can fall in and out of love a dozen times without it being a very serious occurrence. I am a man, and I love you as I have never loved a woman before in the whole of my life!"

His words made the tears flood into Tamara's eyes.

"I ... am not ... worthy of your ... love."

"Is that why you are leaving me?"

She dared not speak, she merely nodded her head.

"What can you have done that makes you say anything so foolish?" the Duke asked. "Or has there been another man in your life?"

She heard the jealousy in his voice and, because she could not bear him to think that was her reason for leaving him, she said quickly:

"There has . . . never been anyone else . . . and there never . . . will be."

"Now that you have said that, do you think I could ever let you go?"

"I have to . . . go!" she said desperately.

There was silence. Then so unexpectedly that she gave a little cry she felt the Duke pick her up from the floor.

He turned her round and held her close in his arms and because there was nothing else she could do she hid her face against his shoulder.

"There is no reason why you should trust me," he said, "and yet I am begging, pleading with you, Tamara, to do so. I have to know why you wish to leave me, why you think, feeling as we do about each other, we could either of us bear to live apart."

He felt her tremble in his arms, and said very softly:

"Tell me, my darling, what you are hiding from me."

"Y.you will be . . . angry," Tamara whispered incoherently.

"I doubt it," he answered. "We have both been angry with each other in the past, but strangely enough it only increased my love for you."

"This is a . . . different sort of . . . anger . . . and if I . . . tell you . . . you will . . . never speak to me . . . again."

She felt the Duke's arms tighten so that she could hardly breathe.

"I am prepared to risk anything rather than lose you."

"When you . . . hear what I . . . have to say . . . you will not . . . mind losing me."

"Are you prepared to bet on that?" he enquired and now again there was that note of laughter in his voice.

Tamara drew in her breath and freed herself from the Duke's arms.

"I . . . I will . . . tell you," she said, "but you must not . . . touch me while I am . . . doing so."

148

"I make no promises as to what will happen afterwards," he said.

She took a glance at his face. But because she could not bear to look at the expression in his eyes, knowing they held the love that she had longed for, she moved away from him.

She stood as he had done at the window, looking out blindly into the sunshine.

She could not see the lake or the trees in the Park because of her tears, but she forced herself to hold some control over her voice as she said softly but clearly:

"I wrote the . . . novel 'The Ducal Wasp'. I am 'T.S.', the . . . author of it!"

It seemed to her as if her voice came back to her from the walls of the room almost as if they echoed every word she said.

Then there was silence – a silence in which she could hear her heart beating. She thought that having heard what she had to say the Duke would leave.

He would walk out of the room and out of her life. She would hear the door close behind him, and that would be the end.

But he did not go and because she longed to run to him and beg him to forgive her, to go down on her knees in front of him and plead with him not to leave her, Tamara held onto the window-sill.

As she did so she forced herself to remember that she had some pride and she must let him go as he would wish.

After a moment, in a different tone from what she had expected, the Duke asked:

"You knew it was libellous?"

"Y.yes."

"And scurrilous?"

"Y.yes."

"And vitriolic?"

"Y.yes."

"You meant it to hurt me!"

"Not . . . exactly," Tamara answered. "I hated you because of what your father had thought about my sister and . . . I believed . . . you thought the same."

"So – it was an act of revenge?"

"Y.yes."

"You must have known that I and other people who read it would recognise it as a portrait of myself."

"It was half-fact, half-fancy. People talked about . . . you, and as I invented the . . . villainous Duke I thought I was . . . paying you back for what your brother had . . . suffered."

"I suppose I understand, in a way," the Duke said slowly, "but it is the sort of book I should not have expected you, or any other woman to write."

"I . . . h.hated you."

"As your eyes told me you did when you first came here."

"When I wrote it, I never . . . expected to . . . meet you or even . . . see you."

"But when you did . . . ?"

There was silence for a moment, before Tamara said frankly:

"I . . . thought that . . . most of what I had said was . . . justified."

"Perhaps some of it was," the Duke said unexpectedly.

Tamara did not answer.

He had not raged at her as she had expected, nor had he been icily sarcastic and caustic as he might have been.

But she thought she had lost his love, and she felt her whole being cry out because she knew that without him she would never be complete again.

'For one wonderful moment I touched Paradise,' she thought. 'Now it is gone and never again will I know such happiness.'

Then she heard the Duke say:

"I suppose you are prepared to make some reparation for

the damage you have done me?"

Tamara made a little helpless gesture with her hands.

"Wh.what can I. do?"

"You could of course, pay me damages."

"You . . . know I have n.no money."

"Then I am afraid you will have to go to prison – and it will be a life-sentence!"

As he spoke she felt him come closer, and even as she turned her head to look at him his arms were round her and he pulled her crushingly against him.

"A life-sentence!" he repeated, "and you will be imprisoned here in the Castle and I assure you I shall be a very severe jailor. You will never escape!"

She felt as if he had suddenly lifted her back into the sky and she was floating in his arms.

"Forgive . . . me," she whispered, raising her face.

He looked at her and she saw there was a smile on his lips.

"I suppose I shall have to," he said, "and we will burn that abominable book together. Then you shall write me another."

His lips were very close to hers as he said:

"Will you write a love-story, my darling? A story of two people who love each other so much that nothing else in the world is of any consequence."

"Are you sure . . . quite sure that is the . . . truth?" Tamara asked.

"I love you!" the Duke said, "and all the books in the world could not prevent me from keeping you with me and making you mine."

His lips came down on hers as he spoke and now he was kissing her fiercely, passionately, demandingly.

The flame that had been awakened in them before rose higher and higher until it seemed part of the sun and the heat of it consumed them both.

"I love you!" Tamara wanted to tell him.

But her heart was singing and anyway it was impossible to speak but only feel that she was part of the Duke as he was part of her.

It was a long time later that the Duke looking down at Tamara's shining eyes and flushed cheeks said quietly:

"How soon will you marry me, my darling? To-morrow?"

"I want to . . . belong to you," Tamara answered. "I will do . . . whatever you tell me to."

The Duke laughed.

"I am wondering how long such submissiveness will last," he said. "I have grown used to fighting for everything I want. I shall miss my most formidable opponent."

Tamara laughed a little uncertainly, then he was kissing her eyes and her eye-lashes which were still wet, her cheeks and again her lips.

As he did so she felt his fingers pulling the pins from her hair. He released it and it fell over her shoulders in a dark red cloud.

"That is how you looked when you were playing with the children in the hay-field," he said. "I have never seen anything so lovely or so desirable."

"You rode away."

"If I had stayed I would have taken you in my arms and kissed you!"

"I felt shy and . . . embarrassed because you had seen me looking so undignified."

He kissed her again before he said:

"I realise how hard you tried to keep me from knowing how lovely your hair is. You pinned it back in that tight bun but still, my precious, you could not hide its colour. It made me long, as I have never longed for anything before, to find the fire in you."

Because of the passion in his voice Tamara once again hid her face against him.

He put his fingers under her chin and turned her face up to his.

"I think I have awakened a little flame," he said, "but my darling heart, I will teach you to burn as I do with a love which will grow day by day and year by year until we are utterly consumed by it."

He kissed her again, then taking great handfuls of her hair which hung nearly to her waist he kissed that too.

"You are so unbelievably beautiful," he said, "that each time I look at you I find you are lovelier than I remembered."

Tamara gave a little sigh of sheer happiness, then said:

"It must be time for the children to get up after their rest. I must make myself look tidy. I would also point out that it is very . . . reprehensible for His Grace the Duke of Granchester to be in the . . . bed-room of a Governess!"

"If you sleep here to-night it will be for the last time," the Duke answered. "After that, my darling, you will be with me."

She blushed at the look in his eyes. Then as she moved from the shelter of his arms she said:

"You are . . . sure you have . . . forgiven me?"

He pulled her back against him as he answered:

"I will forgive you anything in the world as long as you go on loving me. That is all I ask of life, that I should have your love, and that you will never leave me."

There was no mistaking the serious note in his tone and impulsively Tamara put both her arms round the Duke's neck.

"I love you with all my heart and soul," she said. "You fill the whole world . . . there is nothing but you."

His lips, passionate and demanding, took the last words from her lips.

Then as they clung together the door opened and they looked round to see Vava staring at them in astonishment.

For a moment no-one spoke. Then Vava said:

"You are kissing Miss Wynne!"

"No," the Duke replied, "I am kissing your Aunt Tamara."

"How do you know she is my aunt?" Vava asked. "It is a secret."

"You told me," the Duke replied, "when we found you in the wood."

Vava put her fingers up to her lips.

"Oh . . .! That was naughty of me!"

"As a matter of fact," the Duke said picking her up in his arms. "I guessed before you told me. You see, your Aunt Tamara is far too beautiful to be a Governess."

Vava looked from one to the other and said:

"Do you love Aunt Tamara?"

"Very much!" the Duke answered.

"Does Aunt Tamara love you?"

"I think so," the Duke said. "She has promised to be my wife."

Vava put her arms round his neck.

"If you are going to be married," she said, "we shall live here for ever and ever, then I can ride all your horses."

"The whole lot!" the Duke promised, "and have dozens of ponies as well if you want them."

"Oh, really!" Tamara interposed. "You are not to spoil her! She is too greedy as it is already."

"You promised! You promised!" Vava cried. "Oh, Uncle Howard, I do love you!"

She kissed the Duke on the cheek as she spoke and the Duke's eyes were twinkling as he looked at Tamara.

Her eyes met his and she knew they were both thinking that one day they would have children of their own and he would spoil them as now, because he was so happy, he was prepared to spoil his niece.

The Duke put out his hand.

"Let us tell Kadine and Sándor," he said. "I hope they

will be as pleased at the news as Vava is."

"I say, that is jolly fine!" Sándor said when they told him they were to be married. "But I am not exactly surprised."

"What do you mean by that?" Tamara asked.

"Well, I sort of felt that you liked Uncle Howard a lot," Sándor explained, "and after he was so kind to us I had a feeling he liked you too."

"You know too much," Tamara laughed, but the Duke said:

"You are quite right, Sándor, and I think your aunt will make the Castle a very happy place for us all in the future."

"You are quite certain you want us to stay here with you?" Sándor asked. "We would not want to be in the way."

"Of course you will stay," Tamara cried. "We do want them, do we not?"

She looked up at the Duke as she spoke and he smiled down at her with such an expression of love in his eyes that she felt as if her heart leapt towards him.

"I think there is plenty of room in the Castle for two families," he said.

Tamara's face lit up and she said:

"That is almost exactly what Sándor said!"

Tamara looked at the boy as she spoke and Sándor a little embarrassed explained:

"I told Aunt Tamara that I was your heir, but she said you were young and would doubtless marry and have children of your own so I must not count on it."

"I hope you will not be disappointed if I do," the Duke answered.

"No, of course not," Sándor said. "I don't want to be a Duke, all I want is one day to have my own racing-stable."

"I should think that might be possible," the Duke answered. "In the meantime perhaps you would help me with mine."

Sándor looked at him incredulously.

"Do you really mean that, Uncle Howard?"

"You will find there is a lot to do for the race-horses when you are at home in the holidays, and as Abbey is getting old I am thinking of engaging a new trainer. I am sure he would be glad of your assistance."

Sándor gave a whoop of sheer delight. Then Kadine, who had been rather quiet, came and put her arms around Tamara.

"Aunt Tamara, I want to ask you something."

"What is it dearest?"

"If you are going to be married could I please be your bridesmaid? I have always wanted to be a bridesmaid but nobody has ever asked me to be one."

Tamara looked up at the Duke.

"We are going to be married very quietly in the Chapel here in the Castle," he said. "I am quite certain that your aunt will want not one bridesmaid but two, and Sándor of course must give her away."

The children thought this was the most exciting thing that had ever happened and they all talked at once and by the time everything had been discussed over and over again it was time for tea.

The Duke had tea with them and only when the two girls went upstairs to go to bed and Sándor went off to the stables to talk to Abbey were he and Tamara alone.

They walked out through a side-door into the garden, across the lawn and down through the rose-garden.

As they reached the water-lily pond Tamara looked at the Duke and he knew she was thinking of how she had pushed Lord Cropthorne into the water.

"Sándor told me you were laughing when you found him there," she said.

"I laughed," the Duke admitted, "at the same time I was furiously angry! How dare he try to kiss you?"

He put his arm round Tamara's waist as he spoke and drew her close to him.

"I warn you, my darling, that I shall be a very jealous husband. If any man so much as looks at you I will knock him down and if someone like Cropthorne touches you I will murder him!"

Tamara gave a little cry that was very soft and tender.

"Do you really think I would ever want any man to touch me except you?" she asked. "Oh, Howard, you are so magnificent that you make other men in comparison, seem small and insignificant. I love you so overwhelmingly that there is no need for jealousy."

The Duke held her closer still, then he asked:

"How could I have ever had one moment's happiness until you came into my life? There is so much for us to do together, my darling."

"But the first and most important thing is to make the people on the Estate happy," Tamara said. "I should never know a moment's peace if you were ever in any danger again from someone trying to avenge themselves on you."

"You must tell me what I am to do," the Duke said, "and as I have already promised there will be many changes. I have told my farm managers to raise the wages of the labourers and to improve the condition of the cottages."

"Oh, I am glad, so very glad!" Tamara cried.

"It is you who have changed everything, and you will have to help me and guide me," the Duke said.

"That will be easy," Tamara answered, "because Rose told me her mother said that what everyone needed was a touch of love. That is what we have, my wonderful, magnificent husband-to-be and nothing else is of any importance."

"Nothing," the Duke agreed, "except you!"

He looked down into her eyes and said very softly:

"You fill my whole life and you are my hope of Heaven. All I want is your love now and for eternity."

"It is yours . . . completely and . . . absolutely," Tamara tried to say.

But the words were lost against the Duke's lips for he was kissing her fiercely, possessively, passionately, so that she could think of nothing but him.

She felt an ecstasy and a rapture that was indescribable sweep through her body.

It was so vivid, so intense that it was partly a sharp pain.

She pressed herself closer to him, wanting to give him not only her body but her mind, her heart, her soul.

She was trembling and she thought he was too.

Then he carried her up into the starlit sky where there was only themselves and the Divine power which is the very essence of love.

THE END

BARBARA CARTLAND'S 200th BOOK!
NO ESCAPE FROM LOVE

From Barbara Cartland, one of the most romantic and internationally famous writers, comes the thrilling story of a young English girl caught up in the turmoil of Napoleonic France, who finds both romance and danger when she dares to confront the Emperor himself.

This is the 200th dazzling and spell-binding book by the world's favourite romantic novelist.

0 552 10786 7—**50p**

VOTE FOR LOVE
by BARBARA CARTLAND

The Honourable Rayburn Lyle, Under Secretary of State for Foreign Affairs in the new Liberal Government, returns to his house near the Houses of Parliament unexpectedly early. He finds to his astonishment a bomb planted on the hearth-rug of his sitting-room and a woman kneeling near it.

He pulls her to safety but the bomb does not explode and he finds she is a suffragette, He accuses her of trying to kill herself and learns she is Viola Brandon, stepdaughter of Lady Brandon, who supports the famous Mrs Pankhurst and is one of the leaders of the Woman's Suffrage Movement.

How Rayburn saves Viola not once but three times from desperate situations and how their lives become interwoven is the story of this dramatic romance with a background of Suffragette violence.

0 552 10404 3—**50p**

OTHER TITLES BY BARBARA CARTLAND
AND PUBLISHED BY CORGI BOOKS

WHILE EVERY EFFORT IS MADE TO KEEP PRICES LOW, IT IS SOMETIMES
NECESSARY TO INCREASE PRICES AT SHORT NOTICE. CORGI BOOKS
RESERVE THE RIGHT TO SHOW AND CHARGE NEW RETAIL PRICES ON
COVERS WHICH MAY DIFFER FROM THOSE ADVERTISED IN THE TEXT
OR ELSEWHERE.

THE PRICES SHOWN BELOW WERE CORRECT AT THE TIME OF GOING TO
PRESS (MAR 78)

☐ 10786 7	NO ESCAPE FROM LOVE		50p
☐ 10602 X	PUNISHMENT OF A VIXEN		50p
☐ 10549 X	DUEL WITH DESTINY		50p
☐ 10404 3	VOTE FOR LOVE		50p
☐ 10169 9	NEVER LAUGH AT LOVE		50p
☐ 10168 0	A DREAM FROM THE NIGHT		50p
☐ 09757 8	THE IMPETUOUS DUCHESS		40p
☐ 09756 X	BEWITCHED		40p

BARBARA CARTLAND'S LIBRARY OF LOVE

☐ 10543 0	THE HUNDREDTH CHANCE (No 5)	*Ethel M. Dell*	60p
☐ 10560 0	THE REASON WHY (No 6)	*Elinor Glyn*	60p
☐ 10588 0	THE WAY OF AN EAGLE (No 7)	*Ethel M. Dell*	60p
☐ 10624 0	THE VICISSITUDES OF EVANGELINE (No 8)	*Elinor Glyn*	65p
☐ 10644 5	THE BARS OF IRON (No 9)	*Ethel M. Dell*	65p
☐ 10670 4	MAN AND MAID (No 10)	*Elinor Glyn*	65p
☐ 10704 2	THE SONS OF THE SHEIK (No 11)	*E. M. Hull*	65p

*All these books are available at your bookshop or newsagent or can be ordered direct
from the publisher. Just tick the titles you want and fill in the form below.*

CORGI BOOKS. Cash Sales Department, P.O. Box 11, Falmouth, Cornwall.
Please send cheque or postal order, no currency.

U.K. send 22p for first book plus 10p per copy for each additional book ordered to a
maximum charge of 22p to cover the cost of postage and packing.

B.F.P.O. and Eire allow 22p for the first book plus 10p per copy for the next 6 books
thereafter 4p per book.

Name (block letters) ....

ADDRESS ....

(MAR 78) ....